E

TWO MINUTE WISDOM

EVOLVE
TWO MINUTE WISDOM

Radhanath Swami

Tulsi Books

Published and printed by:

Tulsi Books

Tulsi books
(A division of Sri Tulsi Trust)
7, K.M. Munshi marg,
Girgaum Chowpatty,
Mumbai - 400007
www.tulsibooks.com

Evolve is based on various talks given by H.H. Radhanath Swami. This is neither an exact transcription nor an overly corrected version. It is an attempt to retain the spirit of the talk and present the content in a systematic fashion. We hope that the readers will enjoy reading the book and will be enlightened in the topics addressed.

This book is dedicated to
His Divine Grace A.C. Bhaktivedanta Swami Prabhupada.

ISBN : 978-93-81283-01-1

Contents

Introduction

Evolution conveys change, growth and elevation. When seen from a biological perspective it conveys evolution of species from lower to higher abilities. A diametrically different way of seeing evolution is to see it from the perspective of evolution of consciousness.

In biological evolution the change happens externally, but in the evolution of consciousness the change happens internally. Handling external changes is a task of nature and handling internal changes is a task of the spirit. Biologically, evolution may be debatable but in terms of consciousness evolution can be experienced.

'Evolve' is a book which helps us handle and make internal changes and thus facilitate the evolution of our consciousness. 'Evolve' is about growing lotuses in a desert.

How can lotuses grow in a desert? A heart which is fearful of uncertainities, lacks confidence, negative in its approach, always conflicting and having no goal, is like a desert. Even a parched desert can grow lotuses if it rains continuously for days together. This 2 minute wisdom of 'Evolve' is like a incessant shower of rainfall on our hearts. Thus facilitating our desert-like hearts to grow lotuses.

When one learns to overcome fear and tolerates difficulties, he starts living a life of self-confidence and positive attitude. This positive attitude helps him to forgive others for their shortcomings and live with them in unity, thus making life meaningful and making one's own destiny beautiful. This is the series in evolution.

When one does not have wisdom, one behaves like a leaf of a 'touch-me-not' plant, which shrinks its leaves at the slightest touch of a drop of water. The drop of water is compared to calamities that come into our life. When one becomes like a 'touch-me-not' plant, one becomes sensitive to even small provocations. One starts whining at small things, shrinks when calamities come and blasts those who touch him.

'Evolve' deposits a waxy coating of wisdom on the leaf of your life. When one has abundant wisdom, one behaves like a leaf of a lotus plant. The same drop of water which could shrink the leaf of a 'touch-me-not' plant, does not even stay on the surface of a lotus leaf. The drop immediately slides down the leaf. The flow of water does not even leave a scar on the leaf, as if the water never even fell on the leaf. Similarly, for one who has wisdom in his life, calamities do not affect him and they do not even leave scars of nightmare.

Thus evolve signifies the evolution from a 'touch-me-not' leaf to a lotus leaf.

This book will act as a guide for the seeker. Pick it, read it, follow it and feel the guidance of the divine in your lives.

•••

Achieving Self-Confidence

It is well known that self-confidence is a very essential ingredient for success in any field of life. Without such confidence we are afraid to take risks, and we don't have the courage to explore higher horizons while performing our deeds within this world. Real self-confidence is not based on our achievements or our successes in this world but it is based on the fulfillment of who we are, what our purpose is, and what we represent to ourselves, to our families, and to the world around us. If a person has such self-confidence, then he can generate faith and confidence in others.

To fail is not much of a loss, to lose one's character and integrity is a major loss to our inner life. A person with proper disposition and attitude is willing to accept even major failures in the eyes of the world in order to preserve the high values that he or she believes in. If we're willing to sell our ideals, our ethics, our character, our integrity, and our very soul for the adoration of this world, then our so-called self-confidence will be built on a foundation of sand. It has no real substance and it can bring us no real fulfillment.

Reasons For Low Self-Esteem

Low self-esteem is one of the biggest problems in the world not only for the apparently downtrodden people, but even for people in very high positions of control. Low self-esteem really means a lack of real contentment within one's inner life. People with low self-esteem like to gossip. Why? Because that's what gives them pleasure. They do not have any substance inside. On the other hand, self-confident people speak of their ideals in life and not of the faults of others.

A person with low self-esteem is quick to criticize others, whereas a person with some inner fulfillment is respectful to others, and he is naturally longing to show respect to others, to be caring toward others.

A person with low self-esteem is arrogant. He thinks, "I've done this, I've conquered these nations, I've made these millions, I've won these tournaments and so on." Such people are very eager to try to convince other people of how great they are, how successful they are, and what they have accomplished within this world. However, a person with actual self-confidence is humble. Why? Because he simply doesn't need to impress people with cheap words of conceit. If you are actually very weak within you have to brag about whatever great or little things you have done to try to get the approval, the recognition, and the adoration of others. But if you have inner fulfillment, if you have confidence in yourselves, you don't need that.

Once a sage in Himalayas told me that when you do something good and you tell somebody about what you do, then by telling you exhaust most of the credits of what you have done. However, in the world today, we want to take credit for what we have not done, and we want to give blame to others for what we have done. This is another quality of a person with low self-esteem. He makes excuses, and blames others for their apparent shortcomings, whereas a person with self-confidence doesn't make excuses, doesn't blame others, and takes responsibility for what he has done or what he has not done and always strives to improve.

Persons with low self-esteem are dependant on the appreciation, praise, and approval of others, whereas a person with self-confidence is willing to speak what is true and do what is right even if it is very unpopular. Especially for the youth in the world today, association is such a powerful influence. Most people smoke cigarettes, drink alcohol, or do all illicit things, not simply because they really want to do it, but because they want to look cool and be accepted by the people around them. But integrity means we understand what is right and we do it—even if people criticize us, even if people make jokes or laugh at us. Eventually those same people will come to us when they are in trouble, because they understand that here is a person with integrity.

Those with low self-esteem are easily jealous about others success. What is jealousy? That means we are so hollow, so empty within, there is so much lack of fulfillment about our worth, our value, and who we are, that we actually have to feel a type of hatred and jealousy towards others who appears to be better. A person with real self-confidence is the well-wisher of everyone. He is not so concerned with his reputation, but is concerned with his character. He is not so concerned with what he can get and what he can one prove to others by his fashion, by his speech, by the type of furniture he has in his home, but is more concerned with what he is giving to others. Actual self-confidence doesn't mean we become absorbed in our egoistic self. The art of real self-confidence is to become selfless, because in becoming selfless there is inner fulfillment.

Influence Of Upbringing

Many of the problems with self-esteem are due to how we are treated when we are a child. If a parent is harsh towards the child, always criticizing the child, not giving proper encouragement or care to the child, then the child feels worthless, he feels no inner value. If a parent shows love for the child even when they make a mistake, discipline the child but in a way that the child is always assured and reassured of their love, their care and their concern, invest so many encouraging words ten, twenty, thirty times before they'll give one critical word, then the child feels some value. The parent should also teach the child how to make decisions and not depend on others for everything.

In the ancient Vedic texts, there is a very interesting story of a little five-year-old boy Dhruva. His father was the king of the world. Dhruva went through a major psychological trauma. For a little boy his role model is his father. The approval of the father is so deeply meaningful and necessary. So Dhruva just wanted the affection of his father. He was climbing up on his father's lap as he was sitting on the throne. His stepmother chastised him, "You have no right to sit on the throne of your father because you are not born of my womb." Those words were like a cutting dagger to the soft, innocent heart of little Dhruva. He turned to his father but he could not help him. He was devastated, his lips were trembling, tears were pouring from his eyes, he was psychologically disturbed.

Dhruva wanted revenge. He ran to his mother and said, "I want a kingdom bigger and greater than my father." She was a very innocent, simple, and pure-hearted lady. She said, "I've heard that great sages get all their desires fulfilled by worshipping the Lord."

So Dhruva with great determination went into the forest and engaged in severe austerities and the process of chanting God's holy names. After just about five months, he became so purified that he actually saw the Lord standing right in front of him. The Lord told him, "I will give you a kingdom greater than your father or even your grandfather."

Dhruva said, "Now I don't want those things. Seeing You, now I'm feeling inner fulfillment, I'm feeling actual self-confidence. I just want to be the servant of Your servants and never forget You. I just want to live by Your principles. I was looking for broken pieces of glass in the form of fame, power, wealth, and control within this world but I found the rare jewel of inner peace, contentment, and love from seeing You and serving You. I want nothing else." He didn't care what anyone thought. He was only concerned with living by the truth, character, and integrity.

Role Of Faith

So it is very important to understand that real self-confidence is not simply about what we have achieved and what we have conquered, because that kind of self-confidence doesn't bring any real inner accomplishment. Whatever we do, we always have to have more and more. Real self-confidence is when we're actually finding fulfillment and satisfaction with who we are and what we represent within this world. Some fools may think that this type of self-confidence, this type of inner peace, is an impediment to making great strides of achievements in this world. However, the opposite is true. The purer our motives, the greater courage and faith we will have to accomplish things way beyond the horizon of even our imagination. When we have such inner self-confidence, anything we pursue is actually easy. It may be difficult mentally, and it may be difficult physically, but when we have the will, the confidence, and the faith, that makes anything easy.

Bhagavad-Gita teaches that we should be attached to performing our duty but we should not be attached to the fruits of our actions. Success or failure, honor or dishonor, victory or defeat, if we are too much attached and become depressed by failure we can't really succeed.

There is a famous story of a woman named Wilma Rudolf from Tennessee in America. In her early childhood, she had very serious injuries in her legs, which were untreatable by medicine. In fact the specialist doctors told her, "You will never be able to put your foot on the floor for your whole life, you will never be able to take a single step, you just have to confine yourself to a wheel chair till you die."

She was just a little child, but she told her mother, "I want to run on these legs, and be the fastest woman on earth!" The doctors were amused at her imaginations because medically her case had no hope. But her mother told her, "One gets one's abilities from God. Just persevere and have faith and do not be discouraged." It took a couple of years and she was actually able to take off all those medical facilities—cast and everything else that was protecting her foot. She took her first steps and started to walk slowly. Soon she went to school and entered into a race, but she lost. Not only did she lose but she came in last place, way behind everyone else. People were laughing at her, ridiculing her, "What are you doing in this race?" Another race, but again last place, way behind everyone else. Every race last place but she had faith, "I can do great things by the help of God if I persevere."

Some years later in 1960, she won three Olympic gold medals and set world records for running! So her self-confidence was not based upon her successes or achievements; her self-confidence was based on faith in God and her faith in herself—"Whether I win or lose let it be, but I'm going to try."

Confidence In Eternal Self

Every single human being within the world has every reason to find inner fulfillment because we are part of God, we have such wonderful value as human beings. Whether we are big or small we all have the opportunity to do something wonderful. The Lord sees within the heart what is our honesty, what is our ideal, what is our sincerity, what is our integrity. Real self-confidence is based on that sincerity.

Bhagavad-Gita explains that the material elements of this world are earth, water, fire, air, and ether, which are the gross elements, but then there are the subtle elements—the mind, the intelligence, and the false ego. They are all temporary, they are all illusory because our true self is distinct—we are eternal, full of knowledge, full of bliss, we are all part and parcel of the Supreme. That's our real nature. So to build our self-confidence on the foundation of the lower self, ahankara, is foundational to material illusion that is the cause of all suffering. But most people factually build their confidence based on the lower self.

So the real self-confidence that brings inner fulfillment and actually gives us real courage to do the right thing in this world in a wonderful way is confidence in our eternal self—who are we, what is our real purpose in life, why are we here, why are we suffering, and what is really the best thing we can do

for ourselves, our families, and for the world. The soul by nature -constitutionally and eternally-is meant to love, that's why the world is so mad to express their love, channel this propensity to love towards someone, somewhere, and somehow.

The kind of songs people listen to, the kind of novels people read, the kind of movies people watch, the subject matter of most of them is love stories. People are trying to find some means to find inner satisfaction through expressing this insatiable energy to love and to be loved, which is our nature. Only one who has awakened the propensity to love within the heart can achieve real peace. So as we come closer to awakening that love we're actually making real progress in our life and therefore faith is so very critical.

There is a bee called the bumblebee, they are very big and black, and they have tiny little wings. Now according to scientists it's actually impossible for that bee to fly according to all the laws of aerodynamics because their wings are so tiny and thin and their bodies are so big and heavy. However, they just fly around effortlessly. Because they have faith, they have seen all the other bees flying, so they just fly. But technically, scientifically, aerodynamically-impossible.

Faith is so incredible that when we have faith in the inner higher self, when we have faith in the connection with the supreme energy and power of God, we can do incredible things with complete confidence, enthusiasm, and perseverance. And even if we fail a million times, it doesn't matter because we know we are pleasing the Lord by our efforts.

Endeavor With Enthusiasm And Patience

In China, there is a type of bamboo tree that you have to water everyday. When you plant that seed nothing even comes out of the ground, there is no growth for the whole first year. Now what would you do if you are planting a bamboo tree and water that bamboo tree for 365 days with nice water and there is not even a slightest movement, the second year no movement, the third year no movement, fourth year nothing. Why waste any more water on this lazy tree! Nevertheless, the people have faith. They keep watering the tree and this particular tree in the fifth year, within six weeks, grows some 90 feet!

So, we can understand life very much through

nature. It's not that we always get immediate results for what we do. One of the symptoms of faith is patience. In fact how to combine enthusiasm with patience is a great art because if you don't have enthusiasm nothing will ever happen, but if you don't have faith, you will give up if you do not see immediate results.

Just like raising a child, you don't see many results initially. However, little by little, if you raise a child with proper disposition and values, your child can grow up and be a leader of humanity, which takes years of patience. The success is not the external appearance that, "I've attained this." Real success is your attitude that you have faith and with that faith if you are doing the right thing you know, "I am doing something wonderful for God and for the world and the results will come and how they come that is beyond my control."

Pandavas remained faithful to Krishna although they were banished to the forest for 12 years, although they lost everything, but they always had faith that whatever is meant to be will be, and they persevered. When proper time came they fought the Battle of Kurukshetra, and ultimately they were the kings. That's enthusiasm and patience. There is no greater self-confidence than faith in the power, the glory, and the grace of the Supreme.

Access Higher Power

The original people that Lord Jesus Christ made into his devotees were simple uneducated fishermen; Peter and Andrew were just fishing. Fishermen are not very intellectual people, they are just very simple people. However, he imbibed within their hearts such faith that they were giving lectures, they were defeating all kinds of arguments, and they were convincing not only common simple people but even scholars to surrender their lives to their mission and their religion. How were they able to do that? That's because we are not the doers.

Krishna tells us in Bhagavad-Gita, "I'm the ability in man, I'm the strength of the strong, and I'm the intelligence of the intelligent." If we can just be instruments to access that power, that mercy, and that love, what we can do is simply incredible. And the hope to just be such an instrument is incredibly wonderful, it's the ultimate fulfillment in life.

Those who don't want recognition, God gives the greatest recognition. That is spiritual logic. If you want to be famous and great, God will make you famous and great, but then He will just cut you right down. However, if you just want to serve with sincerity, God will make you great and famous for the whole world forever. You simply should be sincere.

My spiritual master, Srila Prabhupada, came to the western world with just seven dollars. It took one month on a cargo ship. He was seventy years old, he had several heart attacks, and he had no contacts who were interested in helping him. Practically for almost the first year there was no success. Everything he did was just taken away. He was living in a little flat with somebody and that person went crazy and kicked him out. He was doing some typing of some articles and books, and his typewriter and manuscripts were stolen. He was living unknown and in poverty.

He was writing to India, to politicians, industrialists, other saints, well-wishers, and pious people. But everybody wrote back the same thing "It's impossible, just come back." He had no encouragement from anyone. He was preaching to a generation that absolutely rejected the culture of anyone above them in age. What a difficult situation.

Where did he get the self-confidence to pursue such an absolutely impossible mission? Prabhupada had complete confidence, total self-confidence based on his faith, and based on his humility. Krishna tells Arjuna in Gita whether you win or lose that is not important, what is important is that you perform your duty with right attitude. Prabhupada lived Gita and soon he was developing a worldwide movement.

When we have faith in that higher power, it can carry us across oceans of obstacles and we can never ever be discouraged. In Vedic texts, there is story of another five-year-old boy named Prahlada. What self-confidence he had. His father was a very powerful demoniac person and such a confirmed atheist that he actually hated God, hated religion, outlawed it, and severely punished anybody who followed it. However, little Prahlada was fully devoted to God. This outraged his father who decided to kill him. He threw Prahlada off cliffs, threw him in oceans, threw him in fire, poisoned him, and tried to stab him with swords and daggers. But Prahlada was confident and fearless, "Whatever I am doing Lord, it's for You." **This is the universal principle of all real spirituality—this type of faith and dependence on a power beyond our own and**

confidence that's based on the foundation of that faith.

How the Lord protects may be inconceivable to our intelligence, but with faith we can understand it. Faith is not based on blind acceptance. Faith is based on logic, philosophy, and authority. Through such divine faith we can see what is invisible to the eyes, at every moment of everyday; we can strive for what is inconceivable and unapproachable, and attain it.

So this was Prahlada's self-confidence. However his self-confidence was not based on arrogance that, "I am great". His confidence was based on the fact that God is great. Prahlada had complete self-confidence, but you have to be genuinely humble to have that confidence. Sometimes the people in this world are under the misconception that to have self-confidence is to be arrogant, conceited. Yes, that is a type of self-confidence, but lowered self-confidence. You can achieve so much but no inner satisfaction, fulfillment, or love.

If our confidence is in God then we cannot lose, we cannot lose our character and our integrity. It is very important to understand that it is better to fail in the eyes of the world and protect the integrity of your character and the ideals that you hold sacred in your life. That itself is victory. However, if you sell that off for the broken glass of material success, then what have you gained? Something hollow without substance, without meaning, without real inner satisfaction. So if we maintain our ideals with faith and confidence in our own inner value, in our own efforts, in our own sincerity, in our own dignity, and in our connection to the Supreme, then in the end our life will be glorious.

Choose The Right Association

The greatest accomplishments achieved within this world enlighten and illuminate the society rather than further the darkness. The soul is like the brilliant sun and all our egoistic obstacles that come are like dark clouds. If we associate with people who sincerely strive to live by these spiritual ideals, who sincerely try to cultivate faith in the highest truths, who don't hypocritically sell their values off for the cheap distinctions of the world, that association will elevate us. In that association we learn how to cultivate self-awareness, spiritual awareness. Moreover, when we hear the histories of the great personalities, it gives us confidence, and we want to follow their example.

George Washington, the first president of the United States, was the general of the American army who fought against the British to somehow or the other get independance. He said that we must keep the company of people who will inspire character and high ideals. He explained that better than associating with anyone who has low integrity is to just remain alone for the rest of your life. Association is so important. We should associate with people who are sincerely striving for higher values in life, and apply those values to our occupation, to our family, to our whole vision.

A person who has self-confidence and faith is always seeing a positive opportunity in every circumstance that comes upon him and that gives life, enthusiasm, and happiness. **Self-confidence doesn't mean being arrogant. Real self-confidence can be born in a heart that's simple, honest, sincere, and humble, a heart that has confidence in the higher power that can bring us to the eternally liberated state of divine love, and bring us glorious successes in whatever we strive to do with the proper ideals. That is the true art of self-confidence.**

•••

Art Of Tolerance

"The nonpermanent appearance of happiness and distress, and their disappearance in due course, are like the appearance and disappearance of winter and summer seasons. They arise from sense perception and one must learn to tolerate them without being disturbed."

—Bhagavad-Gita 2.14

We are living in a world of dualities. It is a challenge to adjust one's consciousness and maintain integrity while tolerating dualities. A coin has a head side and a tail side. If you want one side, you must automatically accept the other; they are inseparable. The above text from the sacred Gita describes how distress is inseparable from happiness; or success and failure are inseparable.

One of the greatest problems we face in life is that we all want to be in control of our destiny, today and tomorrow, but we are not in control. We lose our beauty, we lose our money, and we lose our physical capacities. It is a humbling experience to live in this world because we are not the controllers.

Pride Cometh Before the Fall

One of the dualities we face is of honor and dishonor. To tolerate dishonor is very difficult. When you are dishonored, you get angry or depressed depending on the person and circumstances. Some people pull out a weapon and declare war against those offenders. Other people just remove themselves from society, go to a lonely place, and cry in depression. How can one tolerate dishonor? It is very difficult. In fact, for one who is honored, dishonor is worse than death. However, even more difficult than that, is to tolerate honor without becoming proud. Saint Paul said, "Pride cometh before the fall." The very integrity of one's humanness is destroyed when there is egotism and false pride.

The consciousness of an elevated person is like the ocean which due to its vast depth, is undisturbed by the changes that may take place. In the rainy season, sometimes rivers are several kilometers wide and pouring huge quantities of water into the ocean. And in summer the rivers may become small streamlets. Does either one disturb the ocean? Not at all, because of the ocean's own volume of depth. Everyone is looking for peace and satisfaction. If we do not find great satisfaction within ourselves, then we are very affected and afflicted by the circumstances surrounding us. The key to real peace is within, not without.

Wealth Vs Happiness

The conscious force within our body, our true self, is illuminating our body and mind with consciousness. When the real wealth of the soul is uncovered, then we enter into the ocean of spiritual satisfaction we are able to tolerate the miseries of material existence.

Some years back while I was in Bangladesh, I read a newspaper that explained how Bangladesh is the poorest nation in the world. Now this is very interesting because according to one survey conducted by the London School of Economics, Bangladesh is the happiest country in the world. By material standards that just does not make sense because the world is in a fever due to the belief that money will buy you happiness. In fact America, which has lots of money, was very low on the happiness scale. How is it that the poorest country has the happiest people? This shows that the promise of satisfaction through acquiring more and more material things does not bring happiness. A happy person is one who is illuminated within, who rejoices within, and who finds satisfaction within.

Great is One Who Can Tolerate

People like to adore great people, and people like to become great in their own way. But what actually is greatness? Is greatness having a lot of money? Some of the most degraded people in the world are millionaires and billionaires. Even very wealthy people are funding terrorism. Is that great? Is greatness fame, being a good singer or good dancer, having a beautiful body, being strong or athletic, or being heroic?

According to the universal principle of all spiritual paths, this one line succinctly describes what greatness is: **"One's greatness has to be estimated by one's ability to tolerate provoking situations."** This is something very important to be understood by all human beings. This one line goes beyond all sectarianism.

It's easy to make a show of being great. However, when you're challenged, or have to face provoking situations, it is actually the test of your character. The great scriptures give us this as a constant theme. There are enemies existing within our heart, which are provoked by circumstances both within and without. These enemies are lust, greed, envy, pride, and anger. A great personality is one who is able to tolerate these urges.

Lust

One of the most formidable impulses one needs to tolerate is lust. However, today it is actually quite fashionable, even heroic to succumb to lust. A person is considered manly to the extent he is enslaved and weakened by lust or engages in lusty activities again and again. Isn't that what most movies and television shows are teaching? The greatest heroes are those who give in to their passion or perform tremendously heroic activities in order to fulfill their passionate desires. This is a sign of a much-degraded civilization—that people look up to such inferior mentalities. It is very sad, and we see throughout history how even people in very high and powerful positions are degraded by the provocation of lust. They are unable to tolerate the circumstance.

In the Holy Bible we read that Samson was the strongest man on earth. But Delilah was very beautiful and he lost all of his power, strength, and integrity. Although he could defeat hundreds of men with his bare hands, the beauty of a woman defeated him and he lost everything.

One of the presidents of United States was under severe criticism. He was commander-in-chief of the army, navy, and air force, but not the commander-in-chief of his senses and mind. Marriages are spoilt and nations are put into ruination because people cannot tolerate the provocation of lust.

Anger

When lust is unfulfilled, it brings about a sensation of anger. And what do people do in that frenzied state of anger? When they are upset they say things and do things that sometimes they may regret for the rest of their lives. Anger is very difficult to tolerate.

There is one very inspiring story in Vedic scriptures. There was a king named Rantideva who fasted for a long duration of time for the welfare of the world. When he was on the verge of death, he was brought a large quantity of sanctified food to break his fast. Just as he was about to break this fast, a priest appeared and said, "O Rantideva, I am very hungry. Please give me food." So he fed the priest to his full satisfaction. Then he sat down to eat, and a peasant appeared before him and said, "I am very hungry. Please give me food." Rantideva fed the peasant. Then he sat down to eat, and a person came with a pack of dogs and said, "Rantideva, my dogs are hungry; give them food and water." Rantideva fed the dogs.

All that was left was a little water. If he didn't drink that water immediately, he would die; it was life or death. When he was about to drink that water, a low class person appeared before him and said, "I am very thirsty; would you give me some water?" Would you call this a provoking situation?

Rantideva with folded palms prayed, "My dear Lord, I do not pray to you for mystic perfections, I do not pray to you for salvation from suffering or even liberation. I only have one prayer, "Let me live among all living beings and let me suffer so that other living beings will not have to suffer. In giving this man my water, I will forever be freed from thirst, hunger, moroseness, lamentation, and all the sufferings of material existence." With tears of gratitude in his eyes, he gave the water to that man. That is greatness. That is tolerance.

All of a sudden the priest and all of those personalities who had come to beg from Rantideva, appeared before him, and they all transformed into celestial beings. They gave him nice food and said, "We appeared before you in that way because we wanted to show the world what is a great person."

That is tolerance. One's greatness is estimated by one's ability to tolerate provoking situations. In fact forgiveness and tolerance are inseparable. The power to forgive others for offences and injustices is the actual sign of real tolerance and the quality of a great person. The power to forgive is thousands of times stronger than all the nuclear powers in the world today, because the power to forgive can liberate our soul and liberate so many other souls, which armies, weapons, and entire arsenals of the world cannot do.

Jesus Christ forgave the people who crucified him. His last prayer was, "O Lord, forgive them; they know not what they do."

Greed

Just as from unfulfilled lust, anger arises, similarly when lust is satisfied it creates greed for more and more. Recently in Delhi I was asked to give a lecture in a management institute on "Ethics in Business." People are very disturbed and confused due to unethical behaviour, even from those in very high positions. It is difficult to tolerate temptations. It is very difficult to be honest. Thus it has become just a part of life to take bribes. However, taking a bribe is unethical. You are selling your soul for a little money and degrading the integrity of the whole nation. That is what it is about. When this becomes something normal, we can understand how full-fledged degradation is affecting our world.

In that great scandal of Enron, those people were so wealthy but to get a little more they were cheating the same people who gave their whole lives to make them what they were. What did that do to the morale of the nation? If WorldCom, Enron, and big politicians are causing pain to others just for a little more money or for a lot more money, that is greed. When provoked by greed, people rob, steal, cheat, lie, and even kill. Our colleges must teach students how to follow proper ethics and morality, otherwise afterwards, although they may be big and rich they will simply cause damage to the planet. We can teach theoretically about morals and ethical principles, but unless we have conviction and inner realization, we're very prone to be overcome by temptations for greed.

It is not uncommon to see even governors of states and mayors of cities ending up behind bars, due to being unable to tolerate the temptation of greed. Making extra money in an immoral way ruins lives.

How to tolerate greed? We must understand what real wealth is. Real wealth is in our integrity. Real wealth is in how the Lord within our heart is seeing us. The greatest of all wealth is the wealth of love. Money cannot buy love, fame and prestige cannot buy love. If we are loved and we love, we are wealthy people. And what is the ultimate love? It is the love between the soul and the Supreme Soul, or God.

Envy and Pride

Envy is another enemy existing within our heart that seriously challenges our character. We envy someone who we feel has more than us. It may be more wealth, knowledge, ability, prestige, or high position. Envy is such a deep-rooted disease.

Even among religions we see the provocation of envy on a collective basis in the form of bigotry, sectarianism and fanaticism. Envy and pride are inseparable. We think, "I am a Hindu, I am a Muslim, I am a Christian, I am a Jew, I am a Zoroastrian, or I am a Jain." And because I am that, it means that is the greatest. And if that is the greatest, it makes me the greatest. That's what it's all about.

Every religion has scriptural quotes that say, "We are the way, the truth and the light and there is no other way except through Me." Everyone has their quotes, everyone has their traditions, and everyone has their logic. Even in religious circles, one thinks, "I am the greatest, my religion is the greatest, and everyone else is subordinate or even evil." And we see what this has done to the world today. Religion is supposed to create a sense of seeing every living being with an equal vision. It is supposed to bring a spirit of compassion and love for everyone. If you don't love everyone, you cannot love God. However, religion has the very opposite effect when, it creates sectarianism, bigotry, and hatred toward others. What does that mean? It is an inability to tolerate the envy in our heart in the name of God.

The same problem is seen among nations. Americans think they are the greatest country in the world. When one goes to England, one finds that they also think that they are the greatest, and in Russia, they think that they are the greatest and in France, Greece, Turkey, Iran, Afghanistan, India—every nation thinks that they are the greatest. They hold their flag high. And what is the United Nations? So many flags waving high with each nation thinking “We are great”. And the result is so many wars—territorial wars and egoistic wars.

Envy cannot exist where there is even a trace of real love. Where there is love for God, we see every living being as part of God. And we are happy at another person's success, and sad to see another person's suffering. Although tolerating envy is very difficult, through purification of the heart it becomes natural.

Choice

A tree will stand in the scorching sun to give shade to others. A tree will bear the freezing cold of the winter and give wood to create heat for all. A tree will silently even give up its life to give its body to build a house for others to stay comfortably. That is tolerance. Who is a great personality? One who is more tolerant than a tree. This may seem impossible, but it is actually our nature, our inner nature. Where there is love, spiritual love, there is unlimited tolerance and humility.

There will be many temptations and provoking situations that will come upon us. A very important question for us to contemplate is what do we value as sacred in our lives? Otherwise if we get caught up in the passions of the inner and outer worlds we simply get lost. What is the foundational principle we want to live by- to be a cheater, or a liar, or to give in to lust, anger, greed, envy, and pride? Or is our principle- to be a first class human being, and live with integrity, character, morality and ethics? Happiness comes from fulfillment. Fulfillment is attained when our principles and our lives are in harmony. Hypocrisy creates turmoil and agitation within our hearts.

Gangsters, mafia, and the mob—they are just ignorant and weak. They may have big bodies and big guns; they may control cities or control governments, but they are ignorant weaklings because they are conquered at every moment by their lust, greed, and ego. They have no real substance. They die and then have to pay for all their evil.

The greatest need in human society is people whose lives are good examples. The strongest example is one who lives with dignity and character, because it is so hard to find such people in this world. If we want ethics, character, and integrity to become a sustainable foundation so we can tolerate the storms of life, we must have spiritual realization.

We may be a businessman, engineer, architect, swami, teacher, housewife, or student. Whatever our particular occupation may be, to express our values and our devotion to God and all living beings through our work is the highest and most natural life. In that life there is happiness, and in that happiness we have the power to tolerate all provoking situations.

•••

Forgive And Forget

Forgiveness is a quality that is absolutely crucial for our peace of mind or any peace and harmony within this world because in today's age there is rampant inclination for quarrel and hypocrisy. If we cannot forgive, then there is no possibility of any relationships surviving on any level—whether it is husband and wife, friend and friend, neighbor and neighbor, between castes, between various academic groups, and between nations.

The nature of this world is that it is under laws. Just like there is the law of gravity, which means everything in nature goes down. A structural engineer's whole service is to somehow or other battle against the law of gravity—to build the structure that will stay up despite the natural tendency to collapse. And there are so many impediments to keeping it up. Similarly, there are so many stimulants in this world to drag everything down, especially our consciousness and our relationships. **Without the quality of forgiveness everything sacred in life must collapse.**

Maintaining resentment, hatred, and vengefulness affects our own heart. Someone hurts us and we are angry, we feel that our rights have been violated. It is like picking a burning hot coal and holding on to it day after day, week after week, year after year, with the intention of throwing it on the object of our abuse. Who suffers? We suffer. If we keep this burning blazing fire in our heart, it will burn to ashes all of our virtues, all of our spiritual qualities. It will make us simply miserable. Holding on to these evil intentions towards others is factually—not figuratively but factually—from an emotional, physical, and spiritual point of view, like keeping toxic poisons within our mind.

Any doctor knows that emotional turbulence, especially the poison of hatred and ill intentions toward others, creates emotional and physical disease. Forgiveness is the art of liberating ourselves from that toxic deadly poison that destroys our spirituality, our emotional content, our health, and also potentially of all those who are around us. If we withhold the free choice to forgive someone, we simply remain a victim of whoever has hurt us or abused us. We are really only a victim until we can get that poison out of ourselves through the art of forgiveness.

Real Identity

Now, it's easy to talk about forgiveness theoretically, but how to practice this when our mind and our hearts are in turmoil of various apparent injustices to ourselves? It is important that we understand philosophically the phenomenon that's taking place and also see through historical examples of how others have achieved the goal of this virtue.

We are not these bodies, but spirit soul. This is the first teaching of Bhagavad-Gita. There are eight principle categories of elements within this material nature, from gross elements to the subtle elements. Earth, water, fire, air, and ether compose the gross body. Mind, intelligence, and ego compose the subtle body, which cannot be perceived anyway by the senses, but we know it is there. Gita explains that apart from these gross and subtle natures there is a higher nature—the atma, the soul, which is the source of life, the source of consciousness.

When there is an affliction on the gross body or there is an affliction on the subtle body, which means our false ego, we become terribly disturbed. We are the eternal souls and our purpose in life is to cultivate knowledge and awareness about our true identity. It is simply the illusion and addiction to an untruth that makes us take so very seriously the phenomenal events that come upon our body, mind, and ego. It actually has nothing to do with us, but as conditioned souls, we are habituated so much to want to enjoy through this body. Therefore any affliction that interferes with that enjoyment with the body, mind, and ego causes us terrible pain.

Detachment is a great medicine. That means to identify ourselves with our true essence as the eternal soul that is beyond birth and death. We are the eternal servants of God. **To the degree we are not trying to be enjoyers, or we are actually aspiring to serve rather than exploit, we become transcendental to the various inevitable dualities that come upon us.** We want physical pleasures and prestige. Because of the false ego we have so many expectations. We think we have so many claims of what we deserve and what our rights are. That the more claims you make in life and the more you feel that you expect in life, the more you are going to suffer. Because it does not matter who you are, whether you are simple field worker or whether you are one of the top 10 billionaires in Fortune magazine, it does not make much difference. Things are not going to go your way because we are not the controllers. That power is beyond us.

Correct Understanding

Whoever we are—whether in business, politics, or religion—there are always going to be enemies. There are people who want to exploit you, either intentionally or unintentionally. However, who can exploit us, who can make us a victim? Only those people who actually affect our consciousness. If you are humble and have no expectations, if you make no false claims, then you can actually take everything in a very gracious way.

The soul by nature is pure. Somehow the soul by his own free will has come under the influence of the false ego and according to the modes of nature—goodness, passion, and ignorance—that the false ego decides to associate with, we develop various qualities. Some people are charitable and very concerned with the welfare of others. That is the mode of goodness. But other false egos are under the control of passion, where by hook or crook they must fulfill their greed and lust. If unfulfilled, there is anger, and then delusion. There are those who are in the mode of ignorance, who out of frustration become evil, turn to intoxication, and turn to violence. Actually these are all various levels of disease, but the person that is diseased is the pure soul, a part of God.

Some people may be innocent and basically good but just addicted to all kinds of immoral acts, simply because they just know no better. Others are engaged in horrible activities simply because they have been victimized in their own lives. They may have been abused in so many ways. If you actually look into why a person is doing what he is doing, even if it is bad, if you really study that historically, emotionally, psychologically, you probably would never hate that person. You feel sympathy and sorry for them and hate the acts that they are doing under the influence of the victimization they have gone through. You try to help them, not condemn them.

Sometimes people justify envy, vengefulness, and hatred in the name of God. But it is nothing but their own false ego, not the Supreme Lord God. The God that they worship is their own conceptions of "I and mine," their own self-centered perceptions of life. That's what they live for. People create religions around their false egos. People interpret ancient historical scriptures for the purpose of worshiping, honoring, and serving their false egos. That's what bigotry is, that's what sectarianism is, and that's what terrorism is. This has nothing to do with God. It's imposing our own false ego and all of its hateful intentions in the name of God. **As the heart becomes pure, forgiveness, compassion, and affection manifest as our very nature.**

My spiritual master Srila Prabhupada often said, "Do not blame the instrument of your own karma." It is a fact that whatever is coming upon us and whoever is doing it, they are just instruments of our own karma. We are to blame. Someone has to do it to us. We have to go through it. If a postman comes and hands you a bill of debt of one crore rupees that you owe to a bank, do you attack the postman for that? No. The fact is you took out the loan and you did not pay the loan. So it is your fault. It is not the bank's fault. It is not the postman's fault. You did it. You have a debt and you have to pay it. That's what life is about. It is the laws of nature. For every action there is an equal and corresponding reaction. Or, as Lord Jesus said in Bible, "As you show, so shall you reap."

So whatever is coming upon us, it is the destiny that we have created in our past, and our future is according to how we respond to the karmic reactions that are coming today. If we respond violently, hypocritically, then we are just creating more violent reactions to come to us in future. If we understand that I have to go through this, I have to change, and I should be forgiving to the instrument of my own karma, then we become purified.

Improving Relationships

According to the great saints of all tradition, a definition of love is the capacity to endlessly forgive. The love of parents is that they forgive their child no matter what he or she has done. If they cannot forgive, they do not love. Forgiveness does not mean necessarily that a person should not pay a particular price to learn the lesson. Forgiveness means actually to be the well-wishers, even of our persecutors and thinking in terms of their welfare. Inner peace, Bhagavad-Gita teaches, is to change oneself. Inner peace will never ever come by changing the peace of those who have cheated us or hurt us. We cannot really succeed unless we change our own attitudes and perceptions.

One great thinker has said, "If we do not forgive we are breaking the bridge that we must cross in order to be forgiven for all of the improper things that we have done." We see in this world, in the West, divorce rate is 71% within three years of marriage. We see brothers and brothers fighting with animosity, we see friends and friends, we see people of the same spiritual mission, we see races and races, religions and religions fighting. This inability to make the choice to forgive creates pain, suffering, and chaos. In this world we see it can last generation after generation, even centuries after centuries. People cannot forgive what someone has done to their forefathers a thousand years ago. They still hate and they still want revenge. That is the world we live in.

If we are not a part of the solution we are a part of the problem. William Blake said, "It is much easier to forgive an enemy than to forgive a friend." At first it is difficult to believe, but it is the reality of the world because the more intimate relationship we have with someone, the more we expect from that person. And those expectations are that they will speak and act in a way that I perceive as for my benefit. When you put trust, faith, and affection in someone or they in you, you have the greatest power to cause them pain.

Actually, one time a police officer told me in

United States that they are really not afraid of going into the Mafia dens and breaking things up. What police officers generally fear the most is entering into a scene where there is dispute between loved ones. Why? Because it is such a rage of anger that you have just no idea of what they may do at any given moment. At least with the gangsters, the enemies, the soldiers of the enemy nation, you basically know what they are going to do. Without forgiveness, no relationship can survive. This is a foundational universal principle of all spiritual teachers in all spiritual paths.

Forgiveness Of God And Godly Souls

The Supreme Lord is all-forgiving. He has the power to forgive anyone and everyone of any sins, abuses, and blasphemy. However many of the laws of nature we have broken, the Lord can forgive us in a moment. This is the essence of the scriptures.

sarva dharman parityajya
mam ekam saranam vraja
aham tvam sarva papebhyo
moksayisyami ma sucah

"Abandon all varieties of religion and just surrender

unto Me. I shall deliver you from all sinful reactions. Do not fear." —Bhagavad-Gita 18.66

If He just forgave us without our turning to Him in surrender and love, then we would never learn the lesson and thus we would never enter into the realm of pure love. If we feel the repentance of our misbehavior and are striving to do the right thing in future, then it is the Lord's promise that He will forgive us and restore our eternal and natural goodness.

When God is pleased by our intentions, by the purpose in which we are living, then that affection eradicates all of our past karmas and awakens our innate natural ecstatic love. That is the teaching of the Old Testament, the New Testament, the Koran, the Bhagavad-Gita, and the Puranas—that the Supreme Lord is All-forgiving for those who honestly and sincerely follow His will and depend on His mercy.

The Supreme Absolute Truth is all-forgiving and He has given that power within every living being because we are parts and parcels of the Supreme Lord. Chanakya Pandit said, **"The beauty of a cuckoo bird is its sweet voice, the beauty of a woman**

is her chastity, even an ugly person is seen beautiful if he has knowledge and the beauty of a saintly person is in his power to forgive."

In the Vedic scriptures it is said that qualified brahmins are worshiped by the people in this world because they have the quality of forgiveness. In New Testament Jesus Christ taught his devotees how to pray: "My Lord, please forgive me as I forgive others who have trespassed me." He explained that unless you forgive those who hurt you, God will not forgive you. In forgiving, we are forgiven. Forgiving is the bridge that we must cross to be forgiven. We should not burn down that bridge.

Saint Peter asked Lord Jesus Christ, "If my brother creates very sinful activities against me and hurts me, how many times should I forgive him? Should I forgive him seven times?" Jesus replied, "You should forgive him seventy times seven. It is said, 'An eye for an eye and a tooth for a tooth.' But I say, if someone slaps on your left cheek, you turn your right cheek and say, 'Do it on this too.'" He explains what he means—unless you pray for and love those who persecute you, you will not be seen in a positive light by the Lord. Because if we like those people who like us, that is not a great thing. Even the tax-payers do that. To talk to only those people who are our friends, it is very ordinary. Even atheistic people, who have no moral, will do that. Then Jesus said, "Be thou perfect as your Father in the heaven is perfect. Judge not lest you be judged." He did not just say it. He lived it.

When Jesus was on the crucifix after being beaten, tortured, and blasphemed, just before he entered into state of samadhi, his last prayer was, "My dear father, please forgive them. They do not know what they do." That is a spiritual principle. It is said, **"Forgiveness is the fragrance that a sweet smelling flower like a rose or violet leaves on the heel that has just crushed it."**

In Mahabharata it is described how the Pandavas were exiled to the forest by the envious Duryodhana who tried to kill them and defame them, and he cheated them of all of their rightful property and their service to humanity. He took everything away. They were meant to be living in the palace as kings and queens, but they were just struggling in the forest.

One day Draupadi said to Yudhisthira in a distressed voice, "You are meant to be king. I can't tolerate that you are having to eat some wild fruits and are sleeping on grass. You should be on the throne. This is unbearable. We should go and do something to Duryodhana." Yudhisthira Maharaja replied, "If we become envious, then we have caught the contagious disease of Duryodhana. To be forgiving is real victory." Yudhisthira Maharaja praised him. When we are abused and cheated and we have the power in the core of our heart to pray for the welfare of that person and forgive that person, that is victory. That is the greatness of the person. Duryodhana is sitting on the throne; that's not great. But to have compassionate forgiveness—that is greatness. That was Yudhisthira Maharaja's consciousness.

Perfect Joy

In Italy, near the city of Perugia, is the place called Assisi, the birth place of a very popular saint named Francis. He was the son of a wealthy merchant, but he took up the life of renunciation. Committed to a life of self-imposed poverty, humility, and devotion, he attracted many to follow.

One day he was walking with one brother Leo from Perugia to a very famous temple, St. Maria of the Angel. He was walking for miles and miles, and it was freezing cold. It was raining and snowing. He asked his brother Leo, "I want you to write down whatever I say." They were walking and it was already night time. He said, "What is perfect joy? If our brothers give excellent sermons glorifying our God, I do not consider that perfect joy. If our brothers give sight to the blind, they give ability to the lame to walk and to run, they give ability to the dumb to speak and deaf to hear, and even if they raise a dead man back to life, I do not consider that is perfect joy. Even if our brothers are so deeply learned that they know all philosophy and they know all the science and they have memorized expertly all the holy scriptures, I do not consider that perfect joy. Even if our brothers can prophesize what's going to happen and tell the future and understand astrology and understand the intelligence and the mentality of all species of life and reciprocate with all species in that way, I do not consider that perfect joy."

Brother Leo was surprised and asked, "Then what is perfect joy?" Saint Francis said, "If we can preach the message of God and convert every human being in the entire world to our faith, I do not consider that perfect joy." So finally brother Leo said,

"Francis, please tell me what then is perfect joy?" He said, "When we get to our destination St. Maria of the Angel and it is freezing cold in the middle of the night, we are covered with mud, and it's raining on us, and we are starving of hunger and thirst, and then we desperately knock on the door. Then our brother answers the door and he asks, 'Who are you?' We say, 'We are your brothers, this is Leo and I am Francis. We have come to be with you, to have communion with you. Please give us shelter.' Then he looks up with scorn in his eyes, and says, 'You are not my brothers. You are liars. You are despicable, low grade thieves pretending to be saints. You are exploiting and torturing poor people. You deserve to be punished. Get out from here.' And then he slams the door in our face. I consider that if we bear that and thank God and forgive that man—that is perfect joy."

"Then outside we are suffering so badly and we are freezing, we are starving, we are dying and we are desperately knocking on the door again and he comes to the door and he says, 'Oh, you are back.' We say, 'My brother, we are your brothers. Please show mercy to us, show kindness to us, we are starving, we are freezing, and we are dying.' Then that man becomes so angry, he picks up a big heavy stick, comes out and screams at us, and grabs us by the neck and repeatedly hits us until we are laying in the snow in bloody mess and he just leaves us there freezing, beaten, and blasphemed. In that state, if we could remember our Lord and think, 'My Lord I have tolerated all of this and forgiven this man as an offering of my love to You'— brother Leo, that is perfect joy. **To expect and bear whatever may come into our life and remember the Lord, forgive and love our brother under all circumstances as an offering to the Lord, that is perfect joy.**"

This quality of forgiveness is more illuminating than the light of the sun. Those who have that ability to forgive are invested with the power to access the mercy and the love of God. So, any apparent injustice or setback to us has to be seen as God's arrangement. Not a blade of grass moves without the sanction of the Lord. To tolerate and to maintain the consciousness of forgiveness and compassion means, to pray as a well-wisher of everyone—our friends, our family members, and even our competitors and our persecutors. And thus see every situation as an opportunity to sincerely take shelter of the Lord.

•••

From Fear To Hope

Ushering A New Era Of Change

Mumbai is a sprawling city of around 15 million and much pollution. Behind our shrine, not long ago was a piece of land that was used as a garbage dump. The obnoxious place had heaps of trash with crows and flies swarming about. But that plot has recently been transformed into a sanctuary of trees, flowers, a clear pond, singing birds, and butterflies.

In Mumbai downtown where the temple is, the price of land is exorbitant. People ask, "Why not construct a building on that plot? We could make money. Why a garden?" A primary reason is for the quality of our life. In the environment of ever-increasing stress, it is to provide a peaceful natural place to reflect on the higher values and purposes of life. And more so, this garden is symbolic for our very purpose to transform our heart which is filled with the garbage of lust, envy, and greed into a divine paradise. Lord is in the heart of every living being. When we clear the trash out of our heart and cultivate devotion, our heart becomes a divine abode.

Reality Check

One day, after conducting a seminar, I was sitting on a wooden bench under a palm tree in the garden, watching a butterfly, such a beautiful creation of God. Flapping her wings, she was drinking nectar from flower to flower. I was feeling such peace.

Suddenly through the iron gates some students ran up to me. I could practically hear their hearts pounding. They told me that they were just riding in a train, and a bomb blasted two bogies in front them. In the tangled steel they saw charred bodies hanging and blood streaming. There was a stampede of people running away. There were businessmen and laborers, there were women running with little babies screaming and crying, there were beggars. There was no differentiation. Everyone was running for their lives as police were screaming and ordering everyone to evacuate.

This was the day when there were seven blasts in seven trains in a matter of eleven minutes in Mumbai. Hundreds of people lost their loved ones, thousands got injured, and millions were terrorized.

Everything is temporary, and no one can change material nature. People have fear of terrorism, fear of war, fear of economic crises, fear of disease, and just day to day fears. The World Watch Institute in

Washington DC has given an amazing statistic: from the year 1900 to 1999 there were three times more deaths to human beings caused by war and genocide than from the year 1 AD till 1899. Are things getting better? We like to think so. But in the last hundred years, there have been three times more violent murders than in 1900 years. A Russian writer wrote, **"Through science we have learned to fly in the sky like the bird, we have learned to swim under the water like a fish, but we have not learned to walk on the land as human beings." Martin Luther King said, "Our society has created guided missiles and misguided men."**

Painting of Peace

Once a king had a competition of who could create the best painting which symbolizes peace. One man made a painting which was really a peaceful scene of nice trees, rivers, and birds. It was a very peaceful scene. The other one that was in the final of the competition was a massive storm, where the trees were shaking, where everything was in flux, things were being destroyed, and in one tree there was a little bird that was peacefully singing. The king said, "This symbolizes peace." Because the reality of this world is that there is turmoil and violence everywhere. There is not going to be peace on earth on the material platform. It's never been from the beginning of the history. There are always politics of one person ruling another person, problems and disturbances are constant.

The eternal urgent need for everyone is to understand the peace formula of scriptures. To understand that there is one Supreme Lord. He is the proprietor of everything that exists, and everything is ultimately meant for His enjoyment, and He is our supremely loving well-wisher. One who lives by these principles finds peace within and can spread real peace without. It is beyond all sectarian concerns. This understanding is foundational to real civilization.

There is one beautiful analogy that appears both in Eastern and Western scriptures. If you build a house on shifting sands, in the first storm your house will collapse. But if you build your house on a foundation of stone, it will stand through all storms. This is a world where there are storms inevitably whoever we are? **If we build a foundation in our lives on the basis of truth and real hope in the love of God, then any storm, any situation that may come upon us, we will be at peace, because we experience a higher taste.**

High In Sky - Fearless

One of my dear friends Kevin visited me in New York. His daughter's name is Sally. She is just a little girl, may be two-years-old. Playing with her, he would throw this little girl high in the air, and then catch her. I was really frightened to see it because the floor was made of marble. He would through her way up. He was a very tall person too. I was afraid what will happen if he missed catching her. But as he threw her up, she was smiling and laughing. She loved it. He caught her and threw her again. He did it maybe ten or fifteen times. I was really scared watching it. But he was so expert, he never missed. He always caught her. And little Sally was just enjoying it.

Now if anyone else would have thrown little Sally up like that, she would have been hysterical in fear. Why was she fearless? She was not praying for shelter, she was laughing because she felt complete shelter in the love of her father. It is a fact with children. If children feel deeply loved, they become very fearless and empowered by that love, and if they do not have that love, it is very likely they feel extremely insecure and fearful for the rest of their lives.

We find a similar story in the ancient scriptures in the life of little child Prahlada. His cruel father, wanting to kill him, was throwing him to the bottom of the ocean, throwing in the fire, throwing in a ditch of snakes. Fearless Prahlada, however, was feeling God's love. God's love is to be found within the core of our hearts and when it is found there, we see it everywhere. There is no situation in life or death where the love of God is not for everyone. The path of devotion opens our hearts and opens our eyes to receive it, to perceive it. In that fearless state Prahlada was like that little girl, wherever he was thrown he was feeling the shelter of the loving arms of his supreme father.

Most Optimistic Thought

Though hope helps to transcend fear, but interestingly, misdirected hope is the cause of all fear. We put our hope in the fallible soldiers of this world. We put our hope in our own abilities and abilities of others. But what hope is there? Can anything or anyone in this world save anyone from death? By the power of time, everything and everyone is destroyed.

Does it mean that one should wait for the

hopeless situation to be fearless? Not really. Actually it is hope in the wrong thing that creates fear. Somehow or other if we get the association of godly men, if we cry out for God, then that is a greatly fortunate situation. We all need hope. No matter how bad the situation is, if a person has hope, a person has life, a person has meaning, a person has the spirit of joy that's in that hope.

But for most of us, until we are quite materially hopeless, we do not really take it very seriously. It does not have to be that way, but often it is. We can just understand with good intelligence, where our hope really is. But if we do not act accordingly, then eventually we will be brought to that situation. Everyone is brought to that situation in due course of time—be it rich or poor, man or woman, Hindu, Muslim, Christian, Jewish, Jain, Parsi, atheist, Ph.D., or illiterate. Everyone without exception is brought to a point in life where everything material becomes hopeless. It is at the time of death or before. But if we cultivate within our life with all sincerity, finding hope in the eternal love of God, we will get the full shower of God's mercy.

Once a person came to his mentor and said, "I am feeling hopeless." The mentor replied, "Very good." The mentor then gave an example. "There was a music teacher and he would charge certain fee for people who did not know anything about music, and for people who did, he will charge double. Because he had to unlearn them before he can teach them the right thing." So, before we could really learn how to find hope in God, we have to realize how everything else is hopeless. That is not a pessimistic thought. That is the most optimistic thought.

Nothing to Lose or Gain

All fear is based on two misconceptions—I am this body and those things in relation to this body are mine. This body is temporary and will perish, and all things in relationship to this body will be taken away from us.

The Greek philosopher Socrates not only understood this but he realized it. He was in prison and he was being given poison hemlock. If he drank it, in a matter of minutes he was going to be dead. They said, "Drink this." He said to the people giving, "You cannot kill me because you cannot find me." He was in prison and saying you cannot find me. He had realized that he is the eternal soul. He was fearless.

One Vaisnava saint prayed, "My Lord, my body, my family, my home, my wealth, and my everything are just all Yours. I am Yours, and everything I have is Yours." In that state, you are fearless because you have nothing to gain and nothing to lose materially. He was so filled with God's love. He was self-satisfied, tasting the love of God. "O Lord, if You want, You can kill me; if You want, You can protect me. I am Your servant. You can do anything." That is fearless.

Seek and You Shall Find

The Bible says, "Seek and you shall find." If you have hope in any situation and you are looking for service, there will be an opportunity for service revealed to you. If you are looking for reason to give up your faith, you will find that too. As you approach the Lord, He reciprocates accordingly. If you take full shelter of the Lord, the Lord gives you Himself in full. If you take partial shelter of the Lord, He partially helps and leaves the rest to you.

If we are sincerely trying to taking shelter of God's message, God will give us unlimited hope and unlimited faith in due course. But if we do not have that hope and faith, and we continue with the same sincerity, God sees that we are genuine, we are for real. It is called the dark night of the soul. If you are practicing but you are feeling no love, even you feel your faith waning, but if you carry on practicing, that's the price of divine love.

Currently the love for God in our heart is very external and shallow. We have to sincerely long for that love, and we have to act in such a way that no matter what happens, we are faithful. Then only we experience God's love, and then there is infinite hope and infinite faith, and we become fearless.

•••

Make Your Destiny

"Can we make our destiny? Then, why do bad things happen to even good people?" These topics have been contemplated and debated over millenniums. If God is good, then why does He allow for an apparent injustice, evil, and pain to come upon even people who are innocent?

There was an earthquake in Gujarat in India where thousands of people were killed indiscriminately in a matter of minutes. Hundreds and thousands suffered the loss of loved ones and property, living with lifelong painful injuries, and most of those killed weren't criminal or impious. Some were little children, so young that they had not reached the age where they can reason between good and bad. Why did they have to suffer and die if God is good?

Some years back Ethiopia in Africa was struck with a massive famine, where tens and thousands of people suffered and died of starvation. Amongst them were simple people, even tiny little babies. Even the most apparently kind, generous, charitable, pious people suffering horrible diseases like cancer, diabetes, alzheimer—sometimes even when very young.

During the middle ages in Europe, it was the black plague, bubonic fever, where millions and millions of people died. No one could discriminate who was good and who was bad. Millions died, even small children. If God is good, if God is all-powerful, how and why would He allow this to happen to people who are apparently so innocent?

The disasters of human history—earthquakes, famine, disease, prosecution—create many questions. If God is good, then how could he possibly coexist and do nothing about the evil injustices of this world? This question encapsulates many people's reason for having great difficulty with the idea of God.

Diverse Conceptions

Based on the above apparent contradictions, millions have given up religion, and others trying to somehow or the other hold on to their religious faith have struggled in various ways. After terrible sufferings and deaths of millions of Jewish people in Germany, many Jewish priests evolved theology to a more realistic and practical level where there can be religion and spiritual culture without God—after all, if there is a God and He is good, where was He when all of these people were being tortured and murdered?

Others have struggled with this dilemma in other ways. There are some thinkers, who influence the society much, who claim, "Yes, there must be a God because there must be a cause for everything that exists, but God is not good. God is fundamentally evil."

Others claim that in order to answer this question we have to accept that there are two Gods—an evil God and a good God—God and Satan. The good God is benevolent, compassionate, and is always trying to uplift and help people. And the evil God is promoting so much of injustice, cruelty and suffering. And the competition or the conflict between the good God and the evil God is what existence is.

One philosopher very logically tried to explain how it doesn't make sense to say that there is no God and yet try to have more ideals within society. Because after all if the cosmos is nothing but an accidental by-product of blind evolution, then humanity has nothing to complain. There is no good and there is no evil. We may have our conceptions and our subjective ideas of what is good and evil, but actually everything is just a fact of nature. Without the conception of God, there can be no absolute authority of what is good and evil. Everybody according to their convenience and according to their particular subject could invent what they want to be good and what they want to be bad. Who is to say what's right or what's wrong.

Harold S. Kushner, a Massachusetts rabbi, author of the book When Bad Things Happen to Good People, was from Jewish faith. His young son developed a disease of premature aging, progeria, became very ugly, and died a miserable death. Kushner, who was supposed to be giving faith to thousands of people, had to struggle with the conception of why did God do this to his son? And why did God do this to his people during the holocaust? So his theory, which convinced millions and millions of people worldwide, was that God does exist and God is good but God is not all-powerful. He cannot be all-powerful. If He was powerful, then He would not allow my son to suffer like this. He would not allow injustices to apparently innocent people. The laws of nature are acting and circumstances prevail beyond the control of God. So it doesn't make any real sense, there is no benefit to try to figure out why things happen. It's just circumstances—that's all. God has created the world but He has no power to control what happens within the world.

Although this kept people's faith in God, who may have otherwise become atheists, the problem with this is, it's just not supported by any scripture. Because in the Vedas, in the Christian scriptures, in the Jewish scriptures, God is all-powerful, God is all-mighty. He is not just mighty, He is All-mighty. He is the cause of all causes. He is the efficient cause in which all other causes are relative to. The Absolute Truth is from whom everything emanates. Nothing exists outside God. So if God is all-powerful, the source of everything, the cause of all causes, and nothing exists outside of Him, then why does He allow so much evil and pain within this world?

This is a question that some people just don't want to ask, because it seems so impossible and contradictory. And others give up their faith, or they hold onto a faith that is very superficial and shallow, because they have no answers, or they invent answers that contradict the Holy Scriptures that reveal God.

Need Of Free Will

Vedic scriptures explain this subject in detail. Brahman means the eternal living entity, the soul and Parabrahman means the Supreme Personality of Godhead. The imperishable, eternal, indestructible soul is the source of life, it animates our bodies with consciousness, and it is part and parcel of the Supreme. The Absolute Truth has many diverse energies that are controlling everything. Predominantly there are three—the spiritual energy, which facilitates everlasting, unlimited loving relationships in the spiritual world or the kingdom of God, the material energy, which manifests in this entire cosmic creation; and we, as the part and parcel of the Supreme, are called the marginal energy.

Marginal means we are fragmental spirit souls that are qualitatively one with God—that we are eternal, full of knowledge, and full of bliss—but quantitatively we are only parts. Further, being marginal, we can be under the influence of either the spiritual energy or material energy.

In any case, we are always subordinate to the Supreme, and in that subordination we actually exist for the purpose of love. That is the fundamental need within every living being—to find pleasure, and the ultimate pleasure is the pleasure of loving and being loved. If we don't have that, then all the other sensory pleasures will never satisfy the heart. And the perfect love is the eternal love between the soul and God.

However, in order for love to be real and satisfying, the Supreme Absolute has created every living being with free will. If we don't have free will then we are like robots. A robot can do incredible things but cannot have relationships, cannot love. So it is a necessity for love to be true and satisfying that there be free will. Because it is a quality of God—He is fully independent, so we also have our independence. Therefore, in order to freely love, we must have the freedom not to love.

If someone puts a gun on your head and says, "Do what I say, please me according to my desire," you would probably do it, but are you really happy doing it? Moreover, is that person really happy forcing you to do it? Not really. But if you could do anything—you could beat that person, you could reject that person, you could do anything, but by your own free will you want to please that person, that satisfies the hearts of both, because there is love.

So God has created everything and everyone in such a way that there can be perfect love. Thus He has given us the free will not to love—to accept or to reject.

When the living entity wants to enjoy separate from its loving relationship with God, when the living entity wants to lord it over the resources of material energy, then the spirit soul enters into the material energy and becomes subordinate to the influences of material energy, where there are three modes of nature—goodness, passion, and ignorance. Further, according to the choices we make within this material energy, we identify with this body, and we engage in various activities.

Insuperable Laws

Laws of nature are called the laws of karma. Laws of karma are not subjected to interpretation. They act whether you believe in them or not. Just like there is the law of gravity. If I tell you there is no law of gravity, what goes up doesn't have to come down. Even if I write a hundred thousand volumes of books in eloquent philosophical language to prove and to convince you that the law of gravity is simply created by sentimental fanatics who could not cope with the realities of life, the fact is it is going to go down.

There is the law of action—for every action, there is an equal correspondent reaction. That is scientific. Just like Jesus said so beautifully in Bible, "As you sow, so shall you reap." **The mills of God grind exceedingly fine, but sometimes very slow as well. Whatever you do, whatever you speak, there is going to be a reaction.**

Farmers usually have silos, a storage structure where they put grains from the top and collect from the bottom. Now if a farmer is putting some very cheap, rotten, bad grains in his silo for several seasons, and then he realizes from eating all those bad grains, it's not good for him and his family. Then he starts putting good grains. But what happens? Still the bad grains are there. That means he is suffering for the past. However, in future there is going to be great prosperity because of what he is doing now. Similarly there are people who have been very bad and impious in the past, and they are getting the bad grains of much suffering, but because they are engaging in good activities now, they are putting the good grains on the top, and it's just a matter of time until it all comes upon them as prosperity and happiness.

Man makes his own destiny. God is the cause of all causes because He has created the system, but He gives us free choice within the system. If you take a flight to Calcutta and after it takes off, then you tell the airline steward, "I want to go to Delhi," what is he going to tell you? "You are too late, you are going to Calcutta." You have a choice to do anything, but once you make a choice and do it, you have no choice of what the reaction is going to be. If you cause pain to another by your free will, you have no choice of the reaction. Pain is hundred percent going to come to you—either the same degree or multiplied, depending on your motivation. That is karma.

So, some people may have done activities in their past, and when their sinful karma comes upon them, when suffering comes upon them, are they going to be vengeful? Then they are just accumulating bad karma for the future. However, if we are forgiving, if we are good, what happens is we will pass through the bad karma, and then there will be so much happiness and prosperity in life. That is how the laws of nature work.

There are the laws of state. But you can get away with certain things—you can kill a hundred people but the law of the state is going to kill you only once. The laws of nature, however, can kill you a hundred times or a thousand times or a million times. So the laws of nature cannot be escaped, you can't get around it, you can't bribe. **You cannot buy justice in the law of nature, everyone's equal.**

An intelligent person doesn't simply see through his eyes but he sees through the light of knowledge. If you put poison in a sweet dish it tastes good, but you are going to die. It may take a few days to act, but the poison is there and you have drunk it. So the sinful activities are very pleasing sometimes but the reactions will come. Hence, **it is very important to understand how the laws of karma work, and why they work the way they do.**

Cycle Of Sinful Reactions

In this material nature, according to our activities we are held accountable for everything. According to our activities there are eight million four hundred thousand species of life. In the lower species because of our particular previous actions, we are cast under the control of the three modes of material nature.

The lower species have very little free will. The soul has free will, but it is covered by the ignorance and passion of their previous karmas. Just like you don't see tigers eating grass, and you don't see deer eating rabbits. They are acting according to their nature. They have to evolve through so much enjoyments and sufferings until they finally come to the human form of life which is very rare. After being plants, fish, insects, lizards, birds, animals, and beast, there is the human life.

When we come to the human form of life, it's a very rare and special privilege because in human life the independent free will of the soul can be exercised. In the lower species we are imprisoned by goodness, passion, and ignorance, we are dictated as puppets by the modes of nature. Human life is the prime time where we can make choices. However, because we have this opportunity, we also have responsibility. Everything we say and do, the laws of nature record, and we will get reaction, that is the law of karma.

There are three types of karma according to Bhagavad-Gita—karma, vikarma, and akarma.

1. Karma means good action according to the

scriptures that will bring good results to us. If you are giving charity, you are going to receive manifold more. If you are kind to others, you are going to receive manifold more kindness. That is karma. If you perform proper sacrifices and religious rights, you are going to get good benefits from that.

2. Vikarma means to go against the laws of nature, to engage in sinful activities. Now what happens when we engage in sinful activities? A whole cycle takes place that should be carefully understood. Sinful activity is called as paapam. You engage in sinful activities due to ignorance, the source of all bondage is ultimately ignorance. The eternal spirit soul is meant to love and serve the Absolute, the eternal, constitutional nature of the soul is the source of all the bliss in relation to God. However, we have forgotten. We identify with this body, mind, and the false ego. Moreover, based on this misidentification we act in sinful ways. So, first there is ignorance, and then there are sinful activities.

The reaction of sinful activities is twofold:

i) First is prarabdha, meaning the effect in the form of suffering. You do something wrong and you get a disease, you get put in the prison, you get smashed, people behave with you in such a way that pains your heart. How many ways are there in this universal creation to suffer? There are countless ways to suffer. Why? Because there are countless ways to sin. So prarabdha means we get the suffering results.

ii) The other is aprarabdha, which means 'unmanifested, immature sinful activities.' This is very serious. When you engage in sinful activities you may not get the suffering reaction, that's going to come later, but in the meantime what happens is we create kutam, that means we increase the inclination towards that sinful activity. When we sin, the desire to do that again and again increases. It becomes exaggerated. And when that proclivity becomes very intense, it evolves into bijam, or a specific desire to enjoy through sinful acts. And that sinful desire pushes one, forces one.

Krishna tells Arjuna that the senses are so strong and impetuous that they forcibly drag one down to abominable activities. Then, we again engage in paapam, sinful activities. This again increases our inclination, increases our desire, and we do it again, and eventually we are going to have to just keep suffering reactions again and again. That is vikarma, the vicious sinful cycle. And practically the whole world is entangled in this cycle of sinful activities.

3. Akarma is the third and last type of karma. Akarma means to engage in activities that neither have good or bad karmic reactions, i.e., to engage in transcendental activities or service to God, which is the nature of the soul.

How To Deal With Karma

Laws of karma are often times imperceptible. When we see from the point of view of the soul being eternal and having an ultimate goal, an ultimate destination to achieve, then things begin to make sense. Further, when we understand the transmigration of the soul through various species into this material world, then we can understand a little better. In other words, the suffering that comes on us is not everything at all. It's not the end of the existence. Really, what is it?

Suppose I get malaria, a horrible disease where I get high fever and chills. My whole body becomes very weak. It's a very terrible experience. Now if someone asks me, "Which mosquito bit you? What part of the body? On which date? Where were you?"

I don't know. There is no way for me to know that. However, I know the principle—if I have malaria that means I was bit by a mosquito. I don't know when, I don't know why, I don't know who, but I know I got bit by a mosquito, otherwise I would not have malaria.

Similarly, if we are suffering, we should understand that we would have caused suffering to others, we would have defied our real duties in life as servants of God. We may not know exactly what we did, or when, or how, or to whom, but we know the principle. Moreover, whenever we get malaria, we take the necessary medicine. Similarly when we are suffering, we may not be able to understand exactly why and how, but we know we did something. So take the medicine, and avoid doing those things that will cause it again. That's how we deal with the laws of karma.

Good Vs Bad

In human life, we have the responsibility to discover what's good, and then to do what's good. There's a problem, however, that it's not always easy or convenient to do what's good. In fact sometimes there is a heavy cost to do what's good. You could lose a lot to do with what's good. Because by following the will of God, it seems like the results are pale and abstract, you don't see anything come out of it. You do good, and the results are very abstract. You just have to kind of believe in it, that something in the future is going to happen that's good. But right now you don't see anything.

However, usually when you do evil, when you go against the law of God and act independently, there is immediate tangible result. You work just an ordinary job, you are working so hard, and you get just a little money. But you sell some cocaine or heroin, you will make a million dollars today. That's tangible. That's immediate.

So for this reason, the general tendency of human society is to become influenced by corruption, to go against the laws of God. Especially in today's age, it has become fashionable. Drinking, meat-eating, illicit sex, are considered normal. To be concerned with the lives and happiness of animals and be a vegetarian is weird. To not want boyfriends or girlfriends is antisocial. To not get intoxicated is strange, people will laugh at you. These things are normal even for the biggest politicians and the biggest business people, even sometimes the heads of religions. Why? Because to do good as the will of God is often difficult, inconvenient, and costs a lot, and the results are abstract. However, the result of sin is immediate pleasure, it's tangible: "I can feel it, I can hold it, I can taste it, I can enjoy it." This makes sense, unless we understand the laws of karma.

In every government there are various departments, but they always have a prison department, because however good the government is, whatever benefits they give, there is always going to be people that want to be criminals, that cause suffering to others. So material existence is the prison department of existence, and the purpose is to rectify us. **In our spiritual nature we want to serve the Absolute, but in our conditioned state we want to lord it over, we want to be the proprietor, enjoyer, and the controller. And when you have billions of people, all thinking in this way, can there be peace on earth?**

Conclusion

When so many people are engaging in activities that are violently against laws of nature, then there will not only be crushing results individually but there are going to be cumulative and massive reactions. Because material nature is reacting according to the collective activities of human society, that's why there are earthquakes, that's why there are famines, that's why there are major disasters. Slaughter houses killing hundreds and thousands of God's children every year. Exploiting the resources of the mother earth, polluting the ecology of mother earth, just for greed. People having illicit sex and taking intoxications every day. That's the world we are living in.

God has created the spirit soul, God has created all the species of life, God has created the laws of nature and the reactions, but because we have free will, man is the cause of evil. God simply gives. He is the cause that facilitates us to choose either good or evil. There is no darkness in the sun. If you look towards God, you will see there is only light. However, if you look away from God, then you are going to see darkness caused by your own shadow. **Man creates evil, and evil creates suffering.**

Advancement of civilization comes with spiritual education. Academic education without understanding spiritual values is not going to bring happiness to society. It can bring an artificial superficial sense of prosperity, but people are still going to have to suffer the reactions of their sins. Whether you are suffering in a palace or you are suffering in a straw hut, suffering is suffering. That is why spiritual literatures are so important—to understand who we are, who is God, what is our relationship with God, why we are suffering and how to be free from suffering and experience the greatest happiness—what we are always longing for.

Krishna concludes Bhagavad-Gita with: "Abandon all varieties of religion and just surrender to Me. I shall deliver you from all sinful reactions. Do not fear." This is the universal spiritual principle. Surrendering to the Lord simply means living in harmony with the will of Lord, out of love and affection. This is called akarma, meaning no karma. When we act with conscious desire to please the Lord, He will preserve whatever little we have and give us what we lack. If we simply have that sincerity, the Lord gives us a promise that He will relieve us of all sinful reactions and not only reactions but all sinful desires and all sinful inclinations.

So the most important factor that will help us to make our destiny is how we respond to situations. What is essential is what is our consciousness, what is our aspiration, and what are our values. **If we just** live with integrity, faithful to the principles of ethics and morality, with faith and devotion to God, then we can pass through all these various circumstances and achieve the ultimate destiny of eternal bliss and eternal love.

•••

The Power of Positive Attitude

Every one of us has free will. Life is about how we choose to use our free will at every moment. A thief can take away our money, material nature can take away our health and, time will take away our years. —Everything will be taken away from us inevitably—but there is one thing that no power in all creation can take away our free will. According to how we use our free will, we become conditioned to think in that way, to see the world in that way and to act in that way. We become conditioned by whatever we associate with.

One can use one's free will to smoke cigarettes. No one can force you to do it but the association you keep can severely influence you to do it. When you start, it tastes horrible but by your free will, you keep doing it until your free will is so habituated to surrendering to that experience that you become addicted. Then it practically seems that you do not have free will anymore. By this addiction, you are almost being forced to think, "I have to do it and I have to do it. I must do it. I cannot live without it." Alcoholism and drug addiction work in the same way. You use your free will, you do it enough times and soon you become so conditioned that you willingly surrender to that. It appears that you lost your free will. but in fact, you have not.

However our consciousness is, whatever our way of thinking is, we should understand it is not our nature eternally, it is our acquired nature. It is the nature of the characteristics that we have created ourselves according to what and whom we choose to associate within our lives—, in this life and in our previous lives.

When we associate with people who are positive and when we choose to engage in a positive perspective with positive activities, then we recondition ourselves in that way. This is the special virtue of human life—that we always have a freedom of choice. You may not be able to control the environment but you have full control of how you are going to react to the environment.

If you are on a boat, you may not have control over which way the wind blows, but you do have control over the sails of your boat, and how you are going to respond. You have a choice. When unpleasant or unfair things come upon you, you can either choose to complain or you can choose to learn a lesson. You can be in 'victim consciousness' or you can choose to see what the positive opportunity is in this apparently miserable condition.

Have the Right Perception

Human intelligence is properly utilized when, in whatever situations that come upon us, instead of simply reacting we make an intelligent choice of what is actually the highest virtue that we can achieve. The Bible says, "Knock and the door will open." Every situation is an opportunity. It is said, "When opportunity knocks most people complain about the noise." Vision is to see the invisible, to see the positive possibilities in every situation that comes upon us.

One person says, "Look at this rosebush. It is full of thorns." He keeps on grumbling about the thorns on the rose bush. Another person rejoices, "Look at this thorn bush. It has a rose." They are seeing the same thing. But are they seeing the same thing? No. If you have rose-colored glasses, everything will look rose-colored. If you have yellow-colored glasses, everything will look yellow. If you have green-colored glasses, everything will look green. If you have clear glasses, you see everything as it is. So, according to our state of consciousness, we have certain attitudes, and we will perceive reality according to our acquired attitudes. What attitude we choose to adapt to a situation is what will determine our consciousness and our whole perception of the world.

William Blake said, "We read the Bible day and night. You read black and I read white." We are reading the same words, but according to our attitude we have a completely different idea. Look at the world today. There are people who read the Holy Gita, the Holy Bible, the Holy Koran, the Holy Veda, and when they read it, what do they get out of it? Some people learn to hate and others learn to love. Some people become humble and respectful to all and some people become bigoted, sectarian, and fanatical from reading the same scriptures. Why? It is all based on our association, our perception, and our particular attitude.

If a doctor does not have a positive attitude about curing a patient, will he even try? He will not try with his heart, although may be for some money he may cheat him and say, "I will cure you" when he knows he will not. However, an honest doctor sees the potential to cure the person. So a positive attitude in this case means to see the potential good in someone even if he is in a difficult, miserable situation and actually reach out to help him.

Persevere

Even in this world, if it was not for people with extremely positive attitudes, what we take for granted today would not exist. The first ever academy where I presented a seminar on the philosophy of the Vedas was Wright State University in Dayton, Ohio. This is the place where the Wright brothers were from—Wilbur Wright and Orville Wright. They were farmers and they had an idea that man should fly. Now we take it for granted but in those days it was not possible for them. They were trying to invent a machine that would make man fly, and people thought they were crazy and unrealistic. "Why are you wasting your time? The birds are supposed to fly, ; men are not supposed to fly. Men cannot fly. You are not birds." So they used to criticize them.

They spent hours, days, months, and years working on these machines to fly and absolutely no one respected them, recognized them or thought it was possible. They criticized them. You are fools. You are wasting your time. You are crazy. People would just laugh at them because they kept failing.

People ridiculed them but they persisted year

after year after year and ultimately they flew in the sky, only a few yards. Nevertheless, they actually went up in the air and they saw the potential. And now look at the power of their positive attitude. It may be impossible but it became possible. Why? Because of the power of the positive attitude of people who believed in the ideal of what they were doing and did not care for what anyone or everyone said. They had faith in their ideal. With faith you can see the invisible, you can believe the incredible and you can receive the impossible.

Add the Spiritual Dimension

Modern psychologists approach the attitudes of human beings based on the idea that a human being is a biological and mental being. Therefore they psychologically try to help people to have a positive attitude accordingly, to help people with their physical and emotional conditions. This may be helpful. However, it is incomplete if they do not understand the spiritual dimension of life.

There are eight basic material elements. Five are gross elements—earth, water, fire, air, and ether.; And three are subtle elements—mind, intelligence, and ego. Besides these inferior elements there is a superior nature, which is the spirit soul, the conscious life force within all living beings. The soul, atma, is sac-cid-ananda, eternal, full of knowledge and full of bliss.

The Gita especially teaches about the spiritual dimension of life and its relationship with the mental, intellectual, egoistic and gross forms of matter. It is the greatest and deepest science of reality. It trains us how to have a positive blissful attitude in every situation that can come upon us, even death. Bhagavad-gita was staged on a battlefield for very symbolic reasons. Arjuna was, against his own will, confronted with insurmountable perplexities despite him being a good man. One common questions is why do bad things happen to good people.? There is a reason for everything. A really good person does not see anything as totally bad. He knows about the bad. He does not just hide from it; he is conscious about it. However, he looks for the good opportunity even in the bad.

Deal with Crises

If we look at the world today there is a lot to be really depressed about—the types of pollution, the way people treat each other, so much rudeness, so much selfishness, so much egotism, and even families are breaking apart. There is a lot of evil in this world. And there is a lot of darkness and cruelty as well as terrorism. There are so many terrible diseases. There is so much poverty. There are earthquakes. There are droughts. There are floods. There are massive forest fires.

A newspaper article stated that several children under 25 who die in India, die by suicide. That is serious. Moreover, that is in a country which is supposed to be very highly cultured. Suicide is the ultimate expression of frustration and hopelessness. It is a growing disease all over the world. So if we objectively look at the world we will naturally be very depressed, if we have a heart, or we can be like an ostrich. It is very interesting how the ostriches deal with crises. When the lion comes to eat the ostrich, the ostrich runs and when he sees the lion coming up behind him, he digs a hole in the ground, puts his head in the ground, and thinks, "Now I am safe." When the fox is coming to eat the rabbit, the rabbit's ultimate weapon is he closes his eyes and just forgets that the fox is there. But the fact is the lion is about to eat the ostrich and the fox is about to eat the rabbit. Closing your eyes or sticking your head in a hole in the ground is not going to change the situation.

People in the world today , either just do not want to hear about the problems of the world objectively or they just dig their hole in the ground in the form of television or some sport event, or whatever, just to forget it all. Television is very popular. And sporting events are very popular. People do not care so much about who hits the ball or what is happening on the television. People take those things so seriously because they just want to forget the perplexities, the complexities, and the frustrations of life. It is a way of sticking your head in the ground or closing your eyes.

When Arjuna was faced with severe perplexity, he could not close his eyes or stick his head in the ground. He had to face the reality as it was and he became severely depressed. If a clinical psychologist will read Bhagavad-gita and see the symptoms of Arjuna, he will say, this man really needs some medications. He was shaking. His bow fell from his hand and his dark complexion turned white. His mouth dried up and tears were pouring from his eyes. Arjuna was in a hopeless state. He was depressed. Then he decided, that he wanted nirvana." He told Krishna, "I am not going to stay in this battlefield. I am not going to face this crisis. I am going to the mountains. Better I just renounce everything and negate the problems all together. Then I will be in nirvana, peace." However, negation of the negative is not the best solution. In Bhagavad-gita Krishna taught Arjuna bhakti, devotion.

By engaging in positive activities of devotion, one automatically develops spiritual knowledge and is able to easily forsake attachments. Krishna told Arjuna, "Do not be depressed, do not just artificially close your eyes and escape the problems of life. Do not run away and negate them. See the positive opportunity that you have in this situation and work accordingly." That is the teaching of Bhagavad-Gita. Do your work for the welfare of others in a spirit of compassion to others, with consciousness of your relationship with God. That is what scriptures are all about—developing a very positive attitude— not based on just the physical and emotional but the physical, emotional and spiritual.

The depth of our positive attitude is very much determined by how much knowledge we have of our spiritual self. We can be very positive about various opportunities to make money and very positive to never give up despite so many failures to invent something. We can work hard all our life, even against all odds and failures. One famous person said, "Success means one who goes through failure after failure after failure and does not lose enthusiasm." Another person said, "The only time you fail is the last time you try." So in that sense somebody who just works very hard and does not give up hope in what he or she can do is thinking positively. But what happens when old age starts taking away your facilities beyond your control, people you love start turning against you. It could happen. So inevitable circumstances can come upon us that are completely not according to our plan in life and ultimately everyone, whoever we are, has to come closer to death.

Choose the Right Attitude and Association

Some people complain that when you take to spiritual life you are escaping the world, but that is the most ridiculous misconception. We do not want to escape, we want to face it for what it is. But we want to see it in such a way that we see the goodness. We deal with the badness but we also see opportunities to try to do something wonderful according to our capacity. And that brings us bliss. To know that we are trying to actually help brings us inner and true satisfaction, and that takes a positive attitude based on knowledge. As long as we are attached to being the enjoyer of this material energy, and as long as we have selfishness, greed, envy, and pride within our heart, there are going to be so many frustrations because we are trying to exploit. The actual liberated state is one with a service attitude. We do not want to possess, we do not want to exploit, and we do not want to control. But we want to serve. The actual supreme most positive attitude is to serve in all situations with complete faith in God, faith in the goodness of God and seeing the potential in every possible situation. And that state of consciousness comes through association. If we associate with negative people we will become very negative.

I was speaking to a very high-level managing consultant and he said that in a company, even one person who is seriously negative can spoil the whole operation. Just one bad apple can make all the apples turn bad. It is depressing to be with somebody who is negative and complaining. However, in difficult situations when we see somebody is hopeful, enthusiastic, and has a positive attitude, it brings life. It brings enthusiasm. It brings hope and happiness, to associate with those people and to associate with those free choices. They bring us closer to God, increase our faith in God and simultaneously raise our values in life which will transform our hearts.

Some years back, one of my very dear friends, John, departed from this world. He had a very severe disease and physically he suffered for many years. But he was famous by the nickname "Jolly"! He was always laughing. He was always making everyone happy. This is a positive attitude. He told me on many occasions, "Pain may be inevitable but suffering is optional." It is our free choice, whether we want to suffer or not. The pain is there—that may not be a choice. But our attitude—how we are going to perceive it—is optional. We can see it as the grace of God and even though physically we are hurting, we can find deep fulfillment and gratitude and so many lessons to learn, or we can simply suffer. Everything is a matter of choice—what our mood is, or how we are going to interpret a particular situation. And John was grateful.

Better one moment of full consciousness than a

whole long life of just ordinary relativistic mundane consciousness. Human life is meant for quality and to achieve that quality of good character we must have a positive attitude. We must never give up. We must understand what is really valuable in life and cultivate faith through proper activity and association in which we can live by that idea. A great person is a person who lives with integrity. To be truthful with others is honesty. To be truthful to ourselves is integrity. To be truthful to God, and to be honest and without hypocrisy before God is to be truthful to ourselves. That is real integrity. Proper association and hearing positive, enlightening, spiritual subject matter cleanses the heart and awakens a positive outlook that comes from the very depth of the soul. That is the reason we practice spiritual activities. It is not that they are just superstitious and ritualistic. This is a scientific process of cleaning the heart and accessing the beautiful spiritual qualities of our original nature and to live with a right positive attitude.

•••

Stop Worrying, Start Living

There are numberless reasons why we worry within the world we live. We may be worried about our health, about our wealth, about our loved ones and friends, we may be worried about yesterday or tomorrow, we may be worried about environment, the situation in the world and politics. The nature of this world is birth, disease, old age, and death. The nature of this world is everything is always changing, and essentially the biggest problem is we want to control our environment, but the reality is we are not the controllers. Things will go their own way. We can try our best, and to some degree we have influence, but ultimately things are out of our control. So to the degree we are attached to anything or anyone on this worldly platform there will be worries. Attachment brings worry.

The foundation of a building, although externally cannot be seen, is what gives it strength and holds it up. So our mind is stable when it has a strong spiritual foundation. Storms may come, reversals may come, but if we have that foundation of inner fulfillment, we deal with it with a very clear and practical mind, and it does not disturb us. Because we are connected to something that is immortal, we are connected to the truth that is our home. Our real home is where there is comfort, where there is love, where there is affection, where there is happiness, and where there is trust. That is the actual meaning of home.

However, in this world we are like strangers in a foreign land. What is foreign is the conception—thinking that I am someone that I am not. I am thinking, "I am this body." I am thinking, "I am this mind." The body and mind are subjected to unlimited reversals, and ultimately the body gets old and it dies but the atma, the soul, is eternal. The soul is blissful and fully cognizant. So going back home to our real origin and uncovering the secrets of our true selves is the way to come above all this needless worry of this world and find real fulfillment. Whatever happens cannot disturb that fulfillment.

"A person who is not disturbed by the incessant flow of desires—that enter like rivers into the ocean, which is ever being filled but is always still—can alone achieve peace, and not the man who strives to satisfy such desires."—Bhagavad-Gita 2.70

During the monsoon rains, a puddle of water gets bigger and bigger, and during the dry season the puddle of water dries to nothing. It is very much affected with rains. However, the ocean, whether it is the dry season or the monsoon rains, remains the same. What is the difference? The puddle has no depth. Therefore it is completely affected by its environment and circumstances. But the ocean in its own self has enormous depth. On the surface it is affected by the monsoons, but deep down it's not affected at all. It neither grows bigger or smaller.

Similarly, on the surface we have to deal with the things in this world, but if we don't have much spiritual depth, it really can elate us or devastate us with anxiety, misery, and worry. However, a person who finds that spiritual depth, who uncovers the truth within, deals with the things on surface, but nothing can change that fulfillment, nothing can change that meaning, that love which is within.

Our Natural Position

Years ago, I was walking along the seashore, and I saw a little fish lying on the sand. This little fish was in so much worry, desperately flapping. A wave just washed him ashore. Because he was out of his natural element, nothing could make him happy. So I tried to pick up that little fish and throw him back into the ocean. But he was so intensely worrying that every time I picked him up he just flapped so hard that he flapped right out of hand back into the sand. I was his well-wisher trying to save his life but he could not recognize me. Finally, with both my hands, I cupped him and then I threw him as far as I can in the ocean. But then the next wave of ocean left the fish again flapping in the sand. Again I cast him into the water, and again the next wave left him in the sand to die. I was committed to save this fish. I cupped him and went into the ocean carrying him, step by step up to my knees, up to my waist, up to my neck and I had the fish over my head and I threw him as far as I could. The next wave came, but there was no fish.

I watched the next twelve or thirteen waves—no fish. I felt happy to have saved his life. Fish have feelings, they too worry and they too want to live. That fish was struggling and flapping as much as any human being would in that particular moment. I walked down the shore for a few minutes then I saw fishermen coming with a boat. They had stretched the net along the shore. They brought the net in, I looked in the net, and there were hundreds and hundreds of the same little types of fish flapping and about to be put in frying pans. There was nothing I could do.

I was thinking that the saintly people work so hard to make one person God conscious, to put one person back into the ocean of their natural position. But the illusory energy with her net takes people out of their natural position and puts them in this unnatural situation on the sand of material existence. But who are we in actuality?

Three Planes Of Consciousness

Essentially, there are three planes of consciousness—plane of enjoyment, plane of renunciation, and the plane of devotion. In order to survive, our environment is geared toward exploitation. In Vedic literatures there is a beautiful verse that describes 'jivo jivasya jivanam', that those species that have hands, their food is species without hands, those who have four legs, their food is species that don't have legs, like the grass and so forth.

So in the animal species, even when we look at a beautiful natural scene, there is so much competition there. The fish is happy in the ocean because its natural place is in the ocean. Because it is unnatural on the shore, no matter what you do, it can't really find happiness. However, this picture is limited, because even in that ocean, there is a bigger fish that wants to eat it, and it could be eaten at any moment. So, although we may look at the beauty of the ocean, but out there fishes are eating other fish all the time. And birds are killing insects, and cats are killing birds, bigger birds are killing smaller birds, and big animals in the forest are killing little animals. The fox kills the rabbit, the leopard kills the fox, the hunter kills the leopard, and time kills the hunter.

So, there is competition, that's the nature of the world. Why? Because of selfishness, because we put ourselves in the centre. We find conflict all around—conflict among family members, among nations, among political parties within a nation, among religions, among races, among different types of businesses, among different teams of sports, and there is conflict within our own minds. This is world of conflict, because everyone has a different centre.

Now for those philosophers who promote the path of renunciation, it is taught that there can be no peace in this material existence, because everything is temporary, everything is changing, time is going to kill everything. There is so much conflict for survival, for greed, and for everything else, and we are exploiting so many things. So let's get out of this existence completely. They have nothing to do with it anymore, and their goal is like a deep, dreamless sleep, a type of samadhi, where there is no more pain, no more suffering, no more birth and death, there is just deep sleep. You don't even have consciousness of your own identity. Now that's peaceful. In the West, on the graves it says, "Rest in peace." Now, if death was actually the end of everything, you don't exist anymore, so that is quite peaceful.

The problem, however, is that you are going to be reborn, according to your karma. For every action, there is a reaction—that is the law of karma. You may hurt somebody to get ahead but that same type of pain has to come back to you—it's the law, you can't get away with it, either in this life or next. You may get it in this life and get smashed, or you may take your next birth in a terribly horrible situation, but you can't escape, the reactions will come. That's karma. So we want to get out of this karma, we want to get out of all this frustration. So go into the dreamless sleep of samadhi, enlightenment.

However, the third path is devotion, which recognizes that the highest of all solutions is to understand our origin and to live in harmony with that. The Vedanta sutra is the summary study of all the Vedic literatures, and its very first verse says 'athato brahma jijnasa'- now that you have taken this rare and special human life, it is time to enquire about the Absolute Truth. And the next verse explains that the Absolute Truth is from whom everything emanates.

Upanishads explain that the Absolute Truth is the complete whole that is perfect and complete. He from whom everything emanates, the source of everything that exists, who is within everything, and whom everything is within, that is the whole, that is God. That is what we all have in common. That's the centre. When we learn to recognize that, we could actually have harmony within ourselves and create harmony within the world. And what is our relationship with the Absolute Truth—that we are servants, we are meant to serve.

Lessons From Nature

What is the problem with the environment and ecology these days? There are foreboding disasters looming over us unless we make serious changes. I was told by some geologist that within 50 years there will be no river Ganga and no river Yamuna if we don't seriously start changing our policies. They will be totally dried up because of global warming. Now there are many hundreds and millions of people depending on these rivers for survival. In fact, geologists say that some wars were fought over coal, some were fought over oil, but in future there will be wars fought over water. You can't live without water.

If we exploit the environment, we are going to get the reaction. If we serve the environment, we are going to create harmony, we are going to create prosperity. It's all a matter of consciousness. That's why the conception of evolution is very dangerous. Because how does it impel us to improve our character? We understand that ultimately everything is coming from consciousness; it's the basis of everything that exists. God is the ultimate source of consciousness, and we as living entities are basis of our consciousness. Consciousness is the symptom of the presence of a soul.

If we forget our soul and think we are just matter, then ultimately nothing matters. It only matters according to your particular preference. There is no standard of what's right and what's wrong and what's meaningful. However, if we are actually conscious of, "Who am I? What is my relationship with God? What is my relationship with the environment? What is my relationship with every living being?" then we can actually start creating real harmony because that is based on the truth.

Vedic scriptures explain that if you pour water on the roots of the tree, the whole tree is nourished, and if you give food to the stomach, the whole body is nourished. Every part of a healthy body is serving the whole body. The eyes are not just selfishly doing something, the eyes are directing the rest of the body. The hands are supplying to the rest of the body, the stomach is bringing nourishment to the rest of the body, and the nose is bringing oxygen to the rest of the body. Every healthy cell of the body is serving the whole body. That is good health.

Now what is disease? From a philosophical perspective, disease is when selfish and egoistic germs or cells enter the body. They are thinking about themselves. They are not thinking about the whole body. All the cells that are healthy are good cells. They are living for the whole body and supplying for the whole body. But what about a cancer cell? What is a cancer cell doing? It's living for itself. It's eating the other cells. It's fighting a war against the rest of the body. Then all the healthy cells, because they are concerned for the body, they all start fighting against that disease. But the cancer cells are also fighting very hard, and redoubling, regenerating, multiplying, and each one is just about 'me'. Ultimately, if those selfish cells become stronger and stronger, then the cells that are working together for the whole body are ultimately killed and the body dies.

That's what is happening in the world. The world is a body, humanity is a body, and a proper body is one where everyone is focused on feeding the stomach, everyone is focused on serving the whole for the interest of everyone. However, when you have people who are greedy, selfish, and egoistic, they are like cancer cells in this body, and they are creating havoc. People consider energy and power to be very important, but knowledge is much more important. Because if we apply our knowledge in utilizing the energy properly, it can serve the whole body of the world. It can be utilized in harmony with the Absolute, with God. However, if we utilize that same power and energy without proper knowledge of who we are and what our real purpose in life is, it could create disaster.

Further higher than knowledge is love and

compassion because that brings real fulfillment. Real love and compassion brings real harmony to all living beings because we recognize the spiritual essence in everyone. It's like the atomic energy. It took tremendous amount of knowledge to create it. It can do good, or it can be absolutely destructive, depending upon our knowledge, depending upon our love, and depending upon our consciousness.

Selfless Love

The path of devotion teaches us the simple principle that we are all individual, divine, eternal units who are eternally connected to the Supreme Absolute Truth, and we are all meant to serve the Absolute Truth, and in doing so we serve each other. We create real harmony because we have a common purpose. The real world is where everyone is selfless, where everyone loves.

Real love is without a tinge of selfishness. Real love is based on truth, the selfless expression to please God, to be compassionate to all living beings. The spiritual world is a place of eternal happiness. It's a gigantic unlimited family where everyone is there for each other, where everyone loves each other, and everyone can do anything and everything for each other. Why? Because we see everyone in relation to the centre, to God. That is home. The soul is from that place, the soul is of that place.

To take the soul out of that land of selfless love and devotion where God is in the centre is like throwing a fish on the sand, and that's where we are now—on the sand of the shore of material existence. That spiritual world, although far beyond the material existence, is present within the heart of every living being, today, right now. Real happiness is within. Real intelligence is to understand that. To be illumined within, to rejoice within, that's where the ocean is, which is so deep in satisfaction that anything that happens on this external superficial world doesn't really matter so much. We try to deal with it, but it cannot change our fulfillment and our integrity.

There is this external world. Superior to the external world is the body. Higher than the body is the senses. Higher than the senses is the mind. Higher than the mind is the intelligence, and higher than the intelligence is the atma, the conscious force, our true identity. So to find real fulfillment, we must uncover that essential nature of who we are.

The Peace Formula

Gita explains what the peace formula is. It is that the Absolute Truth is the proprietor of everything, the enjoyer of everything, and the best well-wishing friend of every living being. If we simply understand and accept this, there is real peace, because we find God within ourselves, we find that relationship, and therefore we are here for everyone, because we are all connected, we all have the same source, and we are all related on that level.

The greatest problem in this world is the lack of harmony. We can't artificially make harmony just by peace treaties. Real harmony has to be based on truth: what we really have in common, what our real connection to each other is. Then worry too can be utilized for the highest purpose. A person who is connected to the soul and is connected to God, who is finding that deep peace, fulfillment, and love within, worries about other souls. That's compassion, that's higher than not worrying at all.

Mother Yasoda worried for Krishna. Whenever demons attacked Vrindavan, all the cowherd boys, men, and women worried for Krishna, but that worry was an expression of divine love. Similarly, great personalities worry for people in this world who are suffering with birth, old age, disease, and death. Someone may be sick and dying, and if there is somebody who we love, we naturally worry about them, we care for them, and we feel for them. However, the reality is time moves on, they are going to die. We are going to die. It's just the reality of this world. It's just a matter of sooner or later. And the difference between now or 20, 30, 40 years is not that much. **Better one moment of full consciousness than a long life wasted.**

So the path of devotion is the path that transforms the material world into spiritual, through consciousness. Material world is material world; we can't change it on the external level too much. Whatever government, whatever everything else, still everyone's going to die. We want to make the best we can. It's our duty to make the best possible we can, and the best that can be is to facilitate people to get out, to realize the world within.

Socrates was in prison and was told to drink poison, hemlock. He said to the person who was giving him the poison, "You can't kill me unless you find me." Because he was convinced he was not the body but soul, he wasn't scared, he wasn't worried.

But he took all the risks to teach us because he was worried about others. Isn't that amazing? He wasn't worried about himself dying, but he was worried about the people who did not have that realization. Knowing that it was within them, he wanted to help them to understand that.

Jesus was crucified. He didn't have to. All he had to do was to leave the town. They told him what was being planned and he knew, but he just walked right into it. Because he knew this is what he has to do to establish dharma, religious principles, according to God's will. So he may have suffered in one sense, but that suffering was ecstasy, because he wasn't suffering for self but was suffering for others. This is selfless love.

In order for there to be harmony, there has to be a common centre. And there is only one possible common centre, and that is the complete whole or God. We may say humanity is the common centre, but then what about all the little cows who are getting their throats cut and screaming in agony. That's not real harmony. Nationalism may be good, but we have to go above that too, because we may harmonize within our own nation, which itself is very rarely seen, but what about nations outside our own. Are they not our brothers and sisters? They are not, unless we see the common origin.

The Supreme Lord is the seed-giving father for all the living beings. When we recognize our relationship with God, then we recognize our relationship with every living being, and we can actually create harmony. That's the greatest need. **There is no solution to worrying except finding the peace, the love, and the compassion in ourselves and being instruments of that compassion by connecting to that source that harmonizes everything.**

Making The Right Choices

Gita explains that there is a divine nature and a demoniac nature within all of us. Humility, charity, knowledge of the self, compassion, morality, and generosity are divine, and greed, lust, envy, anger, arrogance, and selfishness are demoniac. Every choice we make is making one stronger and the other weaker. Every time we make an immoral choice, we become more addicted to immorality, and every time we make a right choice, we progress towards perfection.

However, how is that possible in the world when all around us there is so much propaganda for selfishness? It's very dangerous if the cancer cells are seen to be the good cells, and the good cells are seen to be the cancer cells. That's what today's age is about—what's religion is taken to be irreligion and what's irreligion is taken to be religion.

So the most important thing needed is to find the spiritual world within ourselves, to find that oceanic peace, happiness, love, and compassion within ourselves, and to be instruments of that within the world. If we find people who share the same common centre—of purifying our hearts, of serving each other, of being kind, compassionate, and forgiving—then that association is like the spiritual world. However, if we become sectarian, then it's not real. If we are really serving the centre together, then we are trying to harmonize in the universal way.

God has many names, God has many forms, God has been revealed in different ways. Knowledge is so important, and through this knowledge and inner purification, God reveals Himself, gives us light, and gives us hope. Then individually and collectively, we can be concerned with the real issues, with the eternal issues, and we deal with the temporary

situations of this world from that platform of the eternal blissful self. From the spiritual perspective, this is how we rise above all this worry, and start living a blissful life of inner fulfillment.

•••

Unity Is Strength

United we stand, divided we fall. This sentence is simple, yet so deep. It conveys the critical importance of unity. But how to create that unity? How to create a common centre that we agree on in a world of such immense ego, competition, and diversity? This is a great challenge, because wherever there is unity, there is great power and strength to create a peaceful situation in society.

Automobile champion Henry Ford revolutionized the industrial world by creating unity. There were others too making automobiles, but he created the assembly line. It is a simple concept, but it was revolutionary. What is assembly line? Where everybody is just working completely in unity with one another, and that was producing cars so radically fast that he became a multi-multi-millionaire, and everyone else followed his way. Through unity, he gave great strength to the whole industrial world.

When things are unified, they are beautiful. What makes music beautiful? Harmony. And what is harmony? Unity. It's not that the violin is playing one thing, and then the flute is playing whatever he wants, and the drums are playing whatever they want, and the guitar is playing whatever he wants. When there is harmony, when all the voices are trying to make one voice—not that "I'm heard," but "we're all heard"—when all the instruments are trying to combine unitedly to make one sound, then that harmony creates such beauty, such musical talent.

In food, what makes nice taste is someone who knows how to blend spices in a very unified way. For some people cooking is just, "Let's throw this in, and let's throw that in!" However, when somebody knows which spice will compliment which spice to make one flavor, then the food is delicious; it is pleasing to the heart and to the taste.

Similarly in architecture, when there is structural construction, every beam is depending on every other beam for its strength, that is unity. There has to be harmony and balance in the design and in the structure. In a machine, if every part of the machine is not working together in harmony with every other part of the machine, there is a breakdown.

Unify on a Higher Principle

It is the law of nature, the law of gravity to push everything down. What goes up must come down. Everything by nature is going in a downward motion. We have to actually fight against this law to find peace, to find sanctity, to find organization, and to find unity in this world. It is a fact. Time disintegrates everything. That is the law of nature. Moreover, in this age of disagreement and duplicity there are so many different types of egos, and every ego thinks in terms of my own interest, my own purpose. Sociologists and psychologists have called the world today the "I society" where everyone is thinking of "I, Me, and Mine." There are so many different interests, so much conflict, and so much tension. For people to be happy, they have to be free from these tensions created by disunity.

On the battlefield, every soldier is completely dependent on all of his comrades. When there are thousands of people shooting guns and bombs at you, single-handedly, what can you do? Your life, your survival is dependent on all the others around you. It is not that you look at your other comrades who are fighting along with you and think, "I don't like the colour of your skin" or "I don't like the things you eat." No. You understand that "I need you and you need me or we perish," that is what war is about. In the front lines, everyone is dependent on everyone else. This world is a place where war is always going on—the battle of good and evil, the battle of sin and piety, of religiosity and irreligiosity, of love and sectarian hatred. We need each other.

In this world, there are so many chapters of Alcoholics Anonymous, Drugs Anonymous, Gambling Anonymous, and numerous others. Actually, these organizations have been very successful in salvaging people's lives. And what is their power? Their power is two things: having the association of each other, and learning together to depend on the power of God, that is beyond their own. **By the unified inspiration of all of us coming together, we can help each other to access a power beyond our own to actually overcome even very great problems.**

Jesus Christ said, "A house that is divided against itself is a house that cannot stand." In fact, Lord Jesus, by his own example wanted to prove this as one as his last lesson to his disciples. At the last dinner that they were taking together, Lord Jesus went to each one of his disciples to wash their feet with his own hands and then dry them with his own cloth. The first of them, Peter, said, "Master, I can't let you wash my feet. I am your servant." Lord Jesus said, "No, you must. I must teach all of you a lesson.

If this is how I treat each of you, then how should you treat each other?" Then Jesus washed the feet of every one of his followers and dried it with his cloth that he was wearing.

A church was having very difficult times. They were just losing members, they were not growing, and everything was just going down. So they approached a very saintly person and said, "Can you tell us how to build the church up again?" This person replied, "I cannot tell you how to build up your church, but I can tell you one thing for sure, that the messiah has appeared as one of the members of your church—that I know for sure. But I can't tell you who he is." So when they heard that, each one of them thought that all the others could be the messiah. So they overlooked one's faults because after all, he could be our saviour. They respected each other, they honored each other, they served each other, they loved each other, and the church grew and flourished because there was such internal unity amongst them.

However, this unity is difficult because the negative energy and influence is literally terrorizing the world and shackling it to evil qualities. It is so easy to find faults with others. No expert person likes to work under somebody. Any slight disagreement, and people no longer want to work together; there is no more united effort. Everyone wants to be an independent master. However, we see in the example of the five Pandava brothers that even though all were individually very powerful and competent, still they were always together. All of them followed the instructions of the eldest brother Yudhisthira. Despite any of the diversities of opinions, they all agreed and united on a higher principle.

Oneness in Supreme Father

Whether you read the Gita, the Old Testament, the New Testament, or any other scripture, we find there is one God, and that one God is the father of all living entities, the mother of all living entities. We are all children. This is reality. This is a universal principle. And we show our love for our father by how we treat our brothers and sisters. No matter how many gifts you give to your father and mother, if you punch your brother in the face, are they going to be pleased with your gifts? No. The gifts that you offer them will be meaningful when they're offered with love, and that love is expressed by understanding the heart of the father and the mother. They love all their children, and there is nothing greater to a mother and father than seeing the children having unity, love, and trust amongst each other.

We see so much diversity, but how to actually find the oneness in all the diversities in this world. After the World War I, "The League of Nations" was created but then there was World War II, so then "United Nations" was made, but still there is so much conflict in this world. Although these various social and political efforts are necessary within society to keep order and try to create some unity, essentially, it can only really be done on the level of truth on the spiritual platform. If we are going to see unity in diversity, we have to understand how we are all unified, how we are all one despite all the apparent differences.

All living entities are all part and parcel of the Supreme; all are children of the same source. The Absolute Truth is from whom everything emanates. We are all spiritual. We are all part of God; we are all brothers and sisters. If your sister has a disease, do you hate your sister or do you hate the disease? If the disease is there, you hate the disease, but you feel compassion, which is a symptom of love, for your sister. There are people acting in very crazy, violent, and unethical ways, but deep within their heart is the atma, the soul, which is pure, which is part of God, which is our brother or sister. In a person who understands the self, there can be no ego, there can be no hatred toward anyone, there can only be love, and towards those who are unfortunate, there is compassion. That is knowledge of the truth. We are all part of God, and when we develop inner awareness of our relationship with the Supreme, then naturally we see every living entity in connection to that relationship. That is the inner unity extending to create unity within the world.

We find according to the scriptures, the greatest power of those who are learned and realized is the power of love and the power of forgiveness. We take so many little things so seriously, we take all of our differences so seriously because we are not aware of our oneness. Oneness does not mean that we are all just one homogeneous, impersonal substance. Our oneness is in our common relationship with the supreme object of all love or God. To understand that oneness, to realize that oneness can create unity in diversity.

The communists tried to create oneness, just one class. However, all over the world they failed in so many ways because you cannot force oneness. There are people who think differently, there are people with different natures, with different inclinations. There is unlimited diversity and variety in this world; we cannot artificially try to make everything one. However, through inner purification, we can understand and realize within ourselves how there is oneness underlying in all the variety, and then we can try to cultivate that. The scriptures advise us to cultivate inner awareness of the Supreme, and understand what God wants of us, and to actively and dynamically live in this world, work in this world with that basic foundational experience in our heart.

Act with Compassion

There is an inner disunity within all of our hearts. The mind is the battlefield. The dualities of life are always competing with one another. From the spiritual platform, while working in this world to do good, we must simultaneously actually realize the art of love, the art of yoga, to be united body, mind, and soul, and with God. Then we can express that inner knowledge, that inner love, that inner compassion in everything we do. Is there anything that is of greater need in the world than that mentality within human beings? Technology is good provided it is in the right hands. If it is in the wrong hands, knowledge and technology could be the most destructive force on earth, and if it is in the right hands, it can do so much good for so many people. So just creating people who can earn, just creating people who can invent, that is not going to help the world in itself unless people become holistic, unless people become united with their own inner spiritual nature and act with dynamic compassion in this world on that basis.

There is a very instructive story in Aesop's Fables. There was a father whose children were always fighting. So he gave them a very nice lesson. He took many sticks, put them together, and tied them up. When they were bound together, he gave them to each son and said, "I want to see you break these sticks," and they were trying, they could not break that bunch of sticks. None of the sons could break a single stick. Then he untied it and took out one stick at a time and each of them was easily broken.

United we stand, divided we fall. Our strength is in our unity. Not only as nations, not only as races, not only as families, but even within religion; and the greater the service we can do to society, the larger we expand this principle of compassion. There is nationalism, then there is humanitarianism—that means for all human beings—but that is limited too. The greatest compassion is for every living entity, even for the animals and the fish and the birds in the sky, to see the unity we have with all of them, even our unity with the trees and the plants. We are all part of God. **We can show our love for God by how we respect, how we serve, and how we love each other. It is the greatest necessity to create a very deep form of real unity. The unity of inner compassion born of unity between the soul and God is the greatest strength on earth.**

On such a fundamental level as marriage, we see so many problems. There is 70% divorce rate within three years of marriage in America, and now it is growing all over the world. How to protect from that? In marriage you may unify on the principle of romance or beauty, but the bodies change. Your attraction to the beauty of a woman or a man does not remain. Moreover, the minds change because two egos will have so many differences. That is why according to religious principles you take a vow. So you have to stay together no matter what because you have made a vow. You have a responsibility to God, you have a responsibility to your children, you have a responsibility to each other, and through that sacrifice of somehow or other tolerating each other and forgiving each other, you actually learn to really love each other much deeper than the love of the glances and the words.

United on the basis of Truth

Same holds true with spiritual organizations too. There were people with whom I was working, but we had nothing in common. In fact, I really did not like them. I could not tolerate them, and they could not tolerate me either; the kind of people that I would never have anything to do with in my previous life, and here I am working hand in hand with them! We didn't get along, but on the basis of spiritual principle we understood we have so many differences—differences of opinions, differences of ways—we didn't agree on anything except one thing—that the goal of life is to love God, and in order for us to love God we have to love each other.

That person became my very best friend after a couple of years; such honour, such respect, such spontaneous affection earned through sacrifice. The strength of unity, when it is founded within the heart on the spiritual level, is the greatest power on earth, a power that can heal, and a power that can remove tension. Unless we remove the tension within ourselves, how are we going to remove it from other people's lives.

We are all inconceivably, simultaneously one and different from God. We are one in quality with God, we are sat-cit-ananda, eternal, full of knowledge, and full of bliss, and God is sat-cit-ananda, but we are a fragmental particle and God is the Supreme Whole. The oneness between the soul and God is in oneness of love, and we are all inconceivably, simultaneously one with one another. We are of the same quality, we are of the same origin, we are all brothers and sisters on the spiritual platform, but we have forgotten that due to ego, envy, and illusion. So there must be a cleansing of these unwanted things so that we could realize the actual oneness despite all the diversity amongst ourselves and be well-wishers, humble, and forgiving.

Love means sacrifice. Love means service. As

long as we have an individual, personal, egoistic desire to enjoy, there is going to be conflict. As long as we think, "I am the enjoyer, and I am the proprietor," that conception will create so much potential conflicts with any other living being, even our own family members. How many family members divorce, and how many family members are fighting in courts over property. The scriptures teach the unifying peace principle—to understand that God is the proprietor and enjoyer of everything, and we are all meant to work together for that purpose. So, if we really want to make a significant difference in this world, then we must be united on the basis of truth.

The art of loving creates the unity which has unlimited spiritual strength, and that is the greatest need in the world today. **Each one of us can make such a difference if we become humble, if we develop a service attitude rather than an exploitative attitude, if we develop the broad mind to see the oneness and to learn to love all living beings. What a difference each one of us could make, and what a difference we could make if we are united on that principle.**

• • •